# BAD BOYS

## A collection of 20 gay erotic stories

## Edited by Lucas Steele

Published by Xcite Books Ltd – 2012
ISBN 9781908086624

Previous publishing credits:
Stud Poker originally appeared in Freshmen magazine, 2007


Printed and bound in the UK

# Contents

| | | |
|---|---|---|
| **Kid Trouble's Dragon** | Jason Haywood | 1 |
| **Film Noir** | Ed Nichols | 14 |
| **Model Me** | Lynn Lake | 23 |
| **Taking the Bait** | P.A. Friday | 33 |
| **Kissing the Gunner's Daughter** | Beverly Langland | 41 |
| **Hiding Out in His Sauna** | Richard Hiscock | 54 |
| **In the Dark** | Jerry Wilson | 62 |
| **Short Orders** | E.C. Cutler | 72 |
| **Lucky Buck** | G.R. Richards | 82 |
| **Dreams Come True** | Amber March | 94 |
| **Stud Poker** | Landon Dixon | 106 |
| **Spangle** | Alcamia Payne | 115 |
| **The Wrong Side of the Glass** | Josephine Myles | 131 |
| **The Stable Hand** | Jasmine Benedict | 137 |
| **Boys of Summer** | Michael Bracken | 154 |
| **A Trip to the Dark Side** | Scarlet Blackwell | 161 |
| **Bless Me Father** | Heidi Champa | 175 |
| **Lock, Cock and Two Smoking Arseholes** | Marcus Swannick | 182 |
| **Looking Out for Trouble** | Elizabeth Coldwell | 197 |
| **Last Minute Treat** | Allex K. Bell | 207 |

## Kid Trouble's Dragon
### by Jason Haywood

'Out of the dark and starry night! Oh, what mysteries have been sealed so tight! From San Fernando to Fernando Del Rey! Step right this way, lay-dees and gentlemen! Step right this way, into the land of the strange, exotic – and, dare I say it? – the *frightening*! Bring your children and your loved ones, lest they berate you in later life for such an uncalled-for lack in their education!'

At least that's what Ted Harker, the flamboyantly dressed and overly theatrical carnival barker used to shout, back when he was still in charge of his eccentric "Old Style Travelling Show! The Ted Harker Circus of Curiosities! Believe me, lay-dees and gentlemen, it is undisputedly *the Eighth Wonder of the Modern World!*"

And it really was a genuine throwback to the 1920s and 30s travelling carnival. All bright colours and flashing electric lights – advertised with gaudy posters which made it look like a second rate *Believe It Or Not* show. Still, for a few good decades it managed to pull the punters in, and financially it kept itself from going under – giving the locals a little thrill before moving on to the next town, and the next after that. It was also where I first met "Kid Trouble, the Tattooed Terror!".

I'd certainly been at a loose end on the Friday evening of that particular July. I'd broken up with my boyfriend, and after an uneventful string of casual sex partners, I was feeling more than a little tired and jaded with the club scene. I also didn't have any desire or interest in touring the local cruising grounds, but I was still desperate for something – *anything* – to take the edge off the boredom. After I'd seen several of the fliers for the annual local fair I decided what the hell, and had headed off to the show ground on the other side of town. With work scarce and not much spare money to go round at the time, I used to go to a lot of the free attractions and just hang out, and this time there was a good possibility of seeing some of the fairground workhands. Often they would be dressed in T-shirts – or sometimes just bare-chested, which was an added bonus – finished off with a snug pair of well-worn jeans which prominently bulged in all the right places.

With only a handful of loose change in my pocket I aimlessly walked around the rides and stands, happy to watch from the sidelines, until I came across Ted Harker's pitch. Out of curiosity, to see if his show was as good as his spiel, I paid my entrance fee to a woman dressed as some kind of magician's assistant, then went through the canvas flaps and into a massive circus marquee. When there had been enough of us to make up a small group of people eager to be entertained, one of Harker's assistants came to guide us around the exhibits. The whole show was very much how I'd imagined it would be – a collection of about a dozen little tents on their own individual raised stages. Guided from one small tent to another, when we'd all settled in front of one, the curtain would rise, revealing the person or thing behind it. The advantage of the raised platform was to allow the audience easy viewing, and to act as an obstacle to anyone in the crowd who might become a little rowdy. Low, yellow-tinted lighting helped to disguise some of the more obvious fakery which had been deployed to fool a gullible crowd, and I'd been more than a little unimpressed with several of the exhibits. The bearded lady, for one, while The Human Lizard appeared to be someone whose skin resembled a bad case of eczema with theatrical green paint sprayed over it. But when it came to looking at Kid Trouble, things suddenly became quite different.

The guide had built him up pretty well, telling us that he was a European man with a mysterious past who'd sold his body to a Filipino island chief as a living work of art. The practice was supposedly outlawed, because on his death he was to be skinned and the hide displayed in the chief's private collection. The skins would also be traded, bought and sold by collectors for incredible amounts of money – depending on the quality of both the skin and the work inked into it. However, the chief had apparently become impatient and supposedly decreed that Kid Trouble should prematurely meet his maker. There was a reward involved, provided his skin remained undamaged in the process. So he was forever on the run from hired killers – or so the guide had said, hence the name Kid Trouble.

After such a build-up his initial unveiling had been a bit of an anti-climax, as when the curtain was lifted at the front of his little tent all we were greeted with was a tall figure standing perfectly still with his back to us. He was wearing a full-length Wild West long rider coat of waxed cloth and leather, which almost came down to the ground. Only the heels of his bare feet and a mop of light brown hair were clearly visible, and he stood like that for a long 30 seconds – his hands pushed into the coat pockets and the collar turned up high. When he finally turned round, he quickly moved his arms from his sides, twitched his shoulders, and the audience – including myself – gasped as the coat fell to the floor. Kid Trouble was revealed in all his glory, standing on a small dais, totally naked except for a discreet posing pouch. But it was his skin which had really taken us completely by surprise. From collar bone down to his ankles, and out to his wrists, his whole gym-worked body was completely covered in tattoos – the designs even disappearing under the dark cloth of the posing pouch. I've always had a thing about good quality tattoos, and the rush of blood to my cock at the sight of this athletic physique and superior needlework almost made my head spin! Yet even during the gasps, the oooohs and the aaaahhhs, Kid Trouble's face remained emotionless and blank. His eyes just kept looking out over the crowd, at some point in the far distance only he could see, and it was clear from his bored expression that he was automatically going through the motions. Then, before any of the audience had any chance of examining him closely, the curtains on his small tented stage closed again and we were hurried on to the next "Thrilling attraction!".

Back outside I checked my money, then went around to the entrance and paid to go in again. Knowing what to expect, I was prepared for the coat to drop away, which meant I could concentrate more on the incredible body art and the fantastically hot body it was indelibly painted on as well. Impatiently waiting for the tour to reach him again, I worked myself to the front of the group, and while everyone else was caught by surprise as the coat dropped away, I did my best to take more of him in.

Rapidly working my way from his legs up to his strongly featured face, I was mesmerised by what I saw. It wasn't like the cheap and soulless small pieces people often had inked onto various body parts, or the silly little

4

cartoonish doodle things I sometimes saw on display. In reality his body had become a massive canvas of styles, techniques, and artistry. Celtic designs mixed and tangled with Maori, while some were Polynesian but with the distinctive Japanese Yoshika colouring. And there, in the centre of his chest, was what looked like an original Hawaiian representation of the butterfly tattoo made popular by the novel *Papillion*.

The whole artistic effect was beautiful, adventurous, and vibrantly full of organic energy, and I must have said something out loud to that effect, because when I re-focused on his face he was looking directly at me, a smile at the corners of his mouth.

Then the curtains closed again, and despite my attempts to stay, I was quickly moved on by two of the showground's security guards.

There was money enough for a third visit. Only this time, instead of the coat routine, when the curtains drew back he was standing side on to the audience without it, giving me a wonderful teasing view of his back, and the way the designs flowed seamlessly over his taut, dimpled buttock. It also gave me an incredible view of the bulging posing pouch, and I could immediately tell from the shape and the line that it wasn't stuffed with anything other than cock. Knowing there was only a limited amount of time I kept on staring, trying to memorise as much as I could, but as the curtain started to close I looked up and realised he'd been watching me all the time. For a second or two I could have sworn he winked at me, but then the curtain finally closed.

I stood in front of the small stage while the others moved off again, trying to regain my breath a little as well as cursing the slightly uncomfortable restrictions of my rock-hard cock trapped in my jeans. Out of the corner of my eye I saw someone come around from the back and move towards me. But instead of yet more of the carnival's security guys heading over to tell me to move on, when I turned my head to get a proper view I realised it was Kid Trouble himself, and he was coming around the display to see me. He was still wearing the long rider coat and his bare feet seemed a little out of place on the wooden duckboard walkways. Up close he smiled once and sounding slightly bemused, he said, 'I don't have much time between performances, but if you fancy a more private viewing then drop by my trailer later on – say about one o'clock?'

I was totally taken aback. 'I, er, yes – yes, I'd like that.'

He grinned broadly, then stepped in close to me for a moment and opened the coat wide for several seconds before turning and disappearing back around the stage again – calling out behind him, 'And by the way, you don't look too bad yourself.'

With two or three hours to kill I just wandered around the grounds, probably half in a daze of confused thoughts, and it took me a while to get one of the carnival people to finally tell me which trailer Kid Trouble used. The only thing I do remember clearly was by the time one o'clock came around my head had been filled with so many fantasies I just didn't know what to expect. The other thing I was really sure about was that my cock had become uncomfortably hard and erect, purely from just thinking about him!

Eventually, when most of the sideshows had shut down completely, I found his caravan and knocked on the door. It opened, and there he was, in a rich gold-coloured Mandarin-style long kimono which completely covered his tattooed body. Tied snugly at the waist, the cut of the material accentuated his shoulders, then down to his flat stomach – the neckline open a little to reveal a teasing glimpse of coloured artwork.

He smiled and offered a hand to help me up into the trailer. 'Come on in. I wasn't sure if you'd turn up or not – most people find some of the work I've had done to be more than a little off-putting. Do you want a drink? I've only got vodka, and nothing to go with it except ice…'

'Vodka rocks is fine by me,' I said, looking around at the way the trailer had been fitted out. Long periods on the road couldn't have been too pleasant, but the trailer was clean, tidy, and deceptively spacious.

Handing me the glass he sat down beside me on the sofa bench and, in a slightly resigned tone, he asked me whether or not I really found him attractive. 'Yeah, I know you paid to go round and see the whole freak show a couple of times, and you certainly seemed to be into the artwork. But when you said I was beautiful did you mean me, or just this?' He pulled open the neck of the kimono to expose more of his tattooed chest and pecs. 'Some people just turn up just for the cheap thrill of it all. They really find the whole idea of full body tattooing to be repulsive but get a kick over looking at it all the same. It's rare to find someone appreciative of the art and also interested in me.'

Looking at his expressive brown eyes, the shock of light brown hair falling down over his forehead, the slightly pointed nose and expressive lips, I felt I wanted to take him in my arms and just hold him tightly. Silently I took his hand and placed it palm down into my crotch, letting it rest firmly on the bulge my cock was making.

He murmured appreciatively, then put both our drinks to one side before taking me by the hand and leading me down to the curtain dividing the trailer.

On the other side was a large, fold-away bed, about the size of a double, and over it had been stretched a very clean, white cotton sheet. Moving away from me a little he slowly he opened the kimono and let it drop to the floor – leaving him almost totally naked except for a thong-like posing pouch, with its drawstring tided over one hip. Beneath the mass of coloured inks I could see that his body was wonderfully muscled and trim, but not overworked, and there was a lithe suppleness and agility in the way he stood and moved. Calm and confident rather than embarrassed and shy in what he did. His chest had been waxed smooth, and sometime in the past he'd had his nipples pierced because discreet chrome rods with rounded ends sparkled a little in the electric light coming through the windows. A quick glance down at the pouch showed me it was already being pushed away from his groin by his rigid cock – yet before I could move to do something about it he climbed onto the bed and calmly laid down in the centre of it on his back. That was when I realised the plain white sheet was there not only to protect the mattress but also as something for him to display himself on.

As calmly as I could without ripping anything I removed my clothing, parted his legs, then moved onto the bed between them, moving on upwards until our faces were level. Resting my chest lightly on his I could feel the strong, dry heat of his body against mine, breathing it in before I kissed him gently, feeling his submission to my tongue and the exciting way his body started relaxing under me. He slowly started to move his hips a little and I felt the wonderful sensation of his rigid cock rubbing up against mine through the material of the posing pouch.

Then, lifting myself up on my toes and hands, I started

to trace the patterns on his body with the wet tip of my tongue, following the whorls and stripes down around his chest, his pecs and nipples – feeling the way they hardened as my tongue flicked and licked at them – the sound of the metal bars tapping against my teeth. Then I was moving further down the trails, the lines blurring as my head went from side to side – whirlpooling into the abyss of his navel before going off again in other directions – crossing and re-crossing the muscles of his stomach and further down his groin until I was finally forced to stop by the waistband of his posing pouch. The cock it restrained seemed long and invitingly thick through the soft material, and despite the underlying smell of talcum powder the musky, hot smell of his cock and balls made me lay my head down beside the shaft and just breathe it all in for a moment. Lazily I slid my hand up his body a little way, letting my fingertips brush over his abdominal muscles and the marvellous way they felt – not ripped and ridged, but tight and great all the same. Then touching him again as he softly moaned and let himself relax into accepting the pleasure I wanted to give him – though also trying to prolong it for as long as possible for the both of us. Finally even I couldn't wait any longer. It was time to release the beast.

Using my teeth I tugged at the drawstring tied over his left hip, pulling the bow apart before bringing myself up into a kneeling position between his thighs. Slowly I lifted the pouch, teasing myself before finally removing the flimsy garment completely, revealing his wondrously tattooed cock and ball sack. His colourful circumcised cock was standing stiff and erect, but where there had once been a mass of hair there was now closely shaven and waxed skin.

Feeling me tense a little at that surprise, he said, 'I

should have warned you I keep myself smooth. With a dozen shows a night it can get a bit sweaty and the last thing I want is to get an itchy crotch in mid performance.' Then, with half a laugh in his voice, he added, 'Plus the dragon doesn't like pubic hair much either.'

Looking down, I focused my attention on his colourfully tattooed cock. Gently grasping the shaft in one hand and cupping his balls in the palm of the other, I slowly followed the images and lines backwards at first until I could clearly see where the dragon's tail started up on his groin. Then back down again, fascinated by how the body snaked and curled itself several times around the pulsing shaft of his cock, and finally realising that the head of a proudly stylised oriental dragon had been tattooed directly onto Kid Trouble's smooth and bulbous cockhead.

With a touch of concern he asked, 'That doesn't put you off, does it?'

Still staring at his incredible cock, all I could say was, 'Are you serious? That thing is fucking beautiful. I'm going to make this dragon breathe more than just fire, believe me.'

Seconds later I was moving one hand firmly up and down his cock while the other tweaked teasingly at his balls – bringing a steady stream of soft noises from Kid Trouble's throat as he lay back on the bed and started giving into the pleasure of it all again. Hearing those sounds, I finally couldn't resist slipping a length of his cock into my mouth, running my tongue around and over the top of it to feel the outline of the dragon's head, flicking it firmly with the tip, and then finally going down further and taking as much shaft as I could manage into my mouth. His hands lifted up and rested on the back of my head, not forcefully, just to become as one with my bobbing and sucking.

With one hand gently wrapped around his balls, softly squeezing and playing with them, I let go of his shaft and slid my other down between us, easing my middle finger until it had worked its way between his arse cheeks. A little more pressure and it was close up and pressed firmly against his arsehole. A little more and it suddenly slipped into him, right up to the third knuckle. That was too much for him, and with very little warning I felt his balls tighten and contract, and then he was pushing his hips upwards, fast and almost uncontrollably, shooting his load into his mouth, once, twice; his spasms rapidly filling it with jism faster than I could swallow, and the next thing I knew I could feeling it trickling out of my mouth back down his shaft and over his balls.

I let him lay there panting for a while as I carefully got off the bed and used my discarded shirt to wipe his come from around my mouth, then set about wiping his softening cock as well. Looking up at me from the bed he reached out and took my still-stiff cock in his hand and gave it several slow strokes before releasing it and rolling himself over onto his stomach.

'I think you need to slip that cock in here.'

I certainly didn't need any further encouragement! Pausing to appreciate the work displayed on his back, buttocks and thighs, I carefully parted his legs a little before getting back on the bed and kneeling between his thighs again.

With both hands I started to fondle and knead his arse, fascinated by the movement of the pictures and patterns under my hands and probing fingers. And the more I pressed and worked at his arse, the more the extent of the tattoo work was exposed – amazing me that not one single piece of his arse had remained untouched by the tattoo artist's needles. I continued my massaging – occasionally letting my thumbs tease down between his cheeks, until, in one movement, I parted them, bent over, and speared his arsehole firmly with my tongue. He let out a soft groan of pleasure, and the more I tongue-fucked him the more relaxed his arsehole became – pushing back a little when I slipped a thumb up inside and gently finger-fucked him for a moment.

Now the time was right. Carefully I brought his legs back together, moving around so I was straddling his upper thighs, then inching forward on my knees so that my achingly rigid cock pushed up and over his arse crack – feeling him wiggle a little beneath me, then putting his hands back down by his sides as he tried to part his own arse and get my cock to slip down to his ring.

Licking the palm of my hand several times I rubbed it over my cock before finally slipping the rigid shaft between his arse cheeks. Gently moving it up and down between them to get it even more lubricated and wet I brought my body up a little until I could feel the head of my prick was pressed hard against his arsehole. Then, very slowly – despite my aching desire to just push myself deeply into him in one – I started to rock back and forth, my cock pressing harder and harder, until it gently broke through and started to enter him. I did my best to control myself, just inching it in a little at a time – in a little further, then back a little; in, then out again. And every time he attempted to push backward I would put my hands on his hips to stop him – making him wait until I was finally in him and I could feel my balls gently bouncing off the base of his arse.

Then I started to fuck him for real. Leaning forward I repeatedly ran my hands and fingertips over his back, down his spine and then around his hips before pulling his

12

arse cheeks apart and thrusting firmly into him. Two, three, four times before I would then start to move my hands back up over his body again – all the while his breathing was becoming heavier and the sounds he was making were getting louder and louder in time with my pounding into him.

After a few moments I could feel the familiar tingling rush grip my balls and I knew it wasn't going to be long before I was going to be coming myself! Reaching upwards to gain a grip on his shoulders I started to physically pull him backwards onto my cock – feeling his hips buck upwards and pushing backwards into my groin in order to get as much of me inside him as he could. Then, in one heady rush of adrenaline and ecstasy I finally let myself go, thrusting forcefully into him as my body jerked and shot spurt after spurt of hot come deep into him!

It was about a week later that the whole carnival moved on, and several days after that – with what little official paperwork I needed to tidy up finally done and sorted – I caught back up with Ted Harker's travelling show. During the day I would help out with the pitches, but in the early hours of the morning I would happily chase the dragon.

## Film Noir
### by Ed Nichols

If there was anything more boring than spending a gorgeous day watching foreign films, I didn't want to know what it was. I could never understand Ben and Xavier's obsession with movies you couldn't even understand without spending the whole time reading. But being in a relationship meant compromise, and that's exactly what I did when the two of them roped me into helping them put on the town's annual foreign film festival, despite my protests. Subtitles just weren't my thing. Give me a good car chase or superhero flick any day. Something I didn't have to think too much about; those were the movies I loved. But dragging Ben and Xavier to them had become a chore. I guess now I understood how they felt.

I was mostly tasked with manual labour, which suited my skill set just fine. The movie house was in some disrepair, and needed quite a bit of work before it would be ready for the festival. I spent a week cleaning, moving boxes, and painting while the boys spent their time finalising details and schmoozing with the local media. Ben was also going to be the projectionist for the festival, while Xavier would be handling ticket sales. Once my jobs were done, I just had to stay out of the way. That was definitely something I could handle.

The day of the festival arrived, and I was exhausted.

The week had been so busy with last-minute projects and emergencies I barely had time to sleep. The theatre was packed full, ticket sales clearly up from the year before. After I cleaned up and packed away a few things, I figured my day was done. I found a spot in the back of the darkened room, and shut my eyes. There was no sense in wasting an opportunity for a little shuteye. After all, there was nothing more I could do now that the movies had started. The theatre was nice and warm; the smell of popcorn and sticky candy filled the air. My tired eyes fell shut and the last thing I remember seeing was some guy in a black turtleneck ranting at his girlfriend about what she made for dinner.

A sudden bump roused me awake; my eyes shot open only to see Ben and Xavier standing over me, both scowling. I tried to lift my arms but I couldn't. I looked down and saw the purple wristbands from the festival securing me to the seat, the plastic looped through the wrought-iron sides of the vintage seat. The theatre was empty, the screen dark. I knew I was in trouble. Big trouble. Ben leant down, putting his hands on my bound forearms, his face close to mine. My mind couldn't help but focus on his soft lips, looking so good curled up in a smirk.

'Enjoy your nap, Scott?'

I swallowed, trying to buy myself some time to think of a good excuse. Nothing was coming to mind, so I just decided to start talking.

'I'm sorry. I couldn't help it. It's no big deal, though. I'm sure no one even noticed I was here.'

Xavier sat down next to me, turning my head to look in my eyes. My breath caught when I stared into his blue eyes, just as it always did. Even after all this time, they both turned my mind to pudding in an instant. Xavier's finger stayed on my chin as he spoke and had me squirming in my seat.

'You were snoring during the featured film. We had to turn up the sound to drown you out. So yeah, Scott. People noticed.'

Ben stole my attention back when he dug his fingers into my arm just a bit. There was nothing I could do to stop him, but I really didn't want to. While the two of them were busy trying to scare me, my cock was stirring in my jeans.

'So, Scott, what do you have to say for yourself?'

I knew Ben expected an answer, but I also knew anything I said would only get me into bigger trouble. Clearing my throat, I decided that the best thing to do was beg forgiveness from my two best boys. Hopefully, my limited charm wouldn't fail me this time.

'Guys, I'm really sorry. It's just this week really kicked my ass. I honestly never thought I'd fall asleep. But it was dark and warm, and come on, those movies were so damn boring. What could I do?'

I was talking so fast, it took me a few seconds to realise my mistake. The two of them looked at each other, both nodding at the same time. I opened my mouth again, trying to do a little damage control.

'That's not what I meant, guys. You know that. I just meant that it was …'

'Shut up, Scott.'

Xavier startled me with his words, his tone never so forceful before. I looked at him, searching his eyes for the big softy I knew and loved, but instead I saw a blank stare. Ben wore the same expression, his eyes impassive as I looked back and forth between them.

'We both know exactly what you meant, Scott. That's why we both think you need a little culture in your life.

So we're going to show you the last movie again. This time, we're going to make sure you stay awake.'

Ben let me go and I watched him leave the theatre. The lights went dim and then to black, the screen flickering back to life as the opening credits started to roll. I tried my hand at reasoning with Xavier one last time, but it was no use.

'This is pointless. I'm never going to like this movie. You know I'm hopeless, Xavier.'

'I wouldn't be too sure about that, Scott.'

He leant in and kissed me, his tongue diving in my mouth, his hands on either side of my face. My wrists fought against the plastic that kept me still, but there was no budging the straps. I heard the other seat next to me creak, Ben clearly back from the projection room. Xavier let me up for air, and I turned to look at Ben. I waited for his lips to cover mine like Xavier's had, but instead, he turned my face back to the screen, speaking directly into my ear.

'Watch the movie, Scott. I think you'll really like it.'

His tongue and teeth played on my earlobe, my mouth falling open as the movie was beginning. It was the guy in the turtleneck, walking down a sidewalk. Some awful music started to play, just as Xavier started yanking at my belt. I looked down at him, but Ben pulled my face back to the screen, not letting my eyes stray from the subtitles that were now on the bottom of the picture. Xavier pushed my pants to my ankles, my thighs rubbing against the soft velvet of the theatre seat. Ben's voice was back in my ear, just as Xavier wrapped his fist around my cock.

'Be a good boy and watch the movie, Scott, and we just might let you come.'

I forced my eyes to focus on the nonsense that was going on in front of me, but my mind was divided. Ben's mouth was on my neck, his fingers tweaking my nipples through the thin cotton of my shirt. Xavier caressed and jerked my cock, teasing me gently with his hand. I again tested my bonds to no avail, just thankful that my hips were free to move as Xavier increased his pace slightly. Ben bit gently into my neck, sucking and pulling with his lips before letting go of my flesh. The movie wasn't penetrating my brain, the pictures not getting past my eyes. I was desperate to close them, to be able to enjoy the sensations fully, but I thought better of it.

I groaned instead, my voice filling the cavernous theatre. Xavier teased my favourite spot, right under the head of my cock, with his thumb, rubbing up and over my slit in a steady rhythm. I tried to push up into his hand, but he kept control of the pace. Barely managing to blink, my eyes were tired and glassy, desperate to look away from the incomprehensible story that was unfolding. All I wanted to do was look at Xavier's hand moving up and down my cock, or turn my head to kiss either one of them full on the mouth. But I knew I couldn't.

It was torture. Every time I got close to the sweet release of coming, Xavier would back off or Ben would distract me with a tickle, keeping me teetering on the edge of madness. I was getting desperate, and I had to let them know it.

'Xavier, Ben, please. I'm sorry I fucked up. Please, can we stop this now? I can't take it much longer.'

Xavier spoke in hushed tones, his hand no longer moving on my cock. He just held me, and I could feel the blood pulsing as he squeezed me.

'We're not nearly done with the movie yet. Gerard still has to tell Nina about his mistress. There's a long way to go yet. Come on, Scott baby. You can hold out, can't you?'

Ben chimed in, whispering so sweetly as he tortured my nipple between his thumb and forefinger.

'Oh, he'll hold out, won't you, Scott? Now stop talking, you two. You're missing the movie.'

I was helpless, completely and utterly. Slumping back against the seat, I let them have their way. Sweat started to bead on my forehead as the screen held my gaze, the yellow words at the bottom of the screen making absolutely no sense at all. My brain was incapable of comprehending another syllable. Xavier's hand started moving again, and I held my breath to try and keep myself under control. I had my doubts that I would be able to hold out until the end of the movie, but it looked as if I had no other alternative.

I couldn't help but sneak a peek down when both Xavier and Ben went to their knees in front of me. My hands curled into fists, the plastic now digging angry red lines into my arms, but the pain only made me hotter and harder. Ben caught me and stared until I looked back up again, forcing my eyes back to the drab scene unfolding for the guy in the turtleneck. I broke the rules again when I felt both of their tongues touching my cock. This time my eyes closed, the pleasure so overwhelming I needed to shut everything else out. I was lost in the feeling of the swirling strokes, but it stopped suddenly, forcing my eyes back open. Xavier and Ben were looking at me, both busting me for not following their instructions. My eyes went back to the screen, hoping to escape any further punishment for not following the rules. They both started laughing, but I didn't dare look back at them.

'Come on, Scotty. The best part is coming up. We're almost there.'

Ben tried to sound reassuring, but I knew he was enjoying my predicament more than he would ever say. I forced myself to watch the movie as they pulled me forward to the edge of my seat, my cock lying helpless and hard against my belly. My pants were soon gone from my ankles, my belt buckle hitting the floor with a clang. There were four big hands pushing my thighs apart, making me completely vulnerable to their every whim. I could no longer make out who was doing what, Xavier and Ben only visible at the bottom of my vision. I didn't know whose mouth was teasing my cock and whose lips were wrapped around one of my balls. And, more importantly, I didn't care. My eyes followed the pictures and words on the screen, but my mind was fully focused between my legs. I wanted more than anything to put my hands through Xavier and Ben's hair, to feel them as they moved. But I couldn't.

They knew me so well, responding to my every reaction, making sure I stayed tantalizingly close to coming, but unable to get what I wanted. Damn them. I tried to stay quiet, so they wouldn't know how close I was to the edge, but I couldn't keep my mouth shut. Every moan was a dead giveaway, and Xavier and Ben backed off accordingly. I dug my head into the soft velvet seat, unable to stay still a minute longer. My hips moved of their own accord, trying to thrust deeper into the hot mouth that surrounded my cock. The climax that was occurring on screen was small consolation to me, as mine was still so elusive. That was, until I felt a saliva-coated finger nudging at my asshole, trying to coax its way inside. My eyes fluttered closed, but just for a moment, as I forced myself to comply with my orders.

'Guys, please. I can't take it any more. Can I come now please?'

The mouth that had been around my cock disappeared and I heard Ben's voice over the sound of the music that was coming out of the theatre's speakers.

'Are you really sorry, Scott?'

'Yes. Yes, I swear. I'm sorry for falling asleep.'

This time Xavier spoke up, sounding like the sweet boy I knew.

'Well, Benny. What do you think? Has he suffered enough?'

'I guess so. Besides, it looks like the movie is over. You can stop watching now, Scotty.'

My eyes dropped just in time to see Ben take my cock into his mouth, and Xavier pushed his finger inside me, his mouth licking my inner thigh. My arms strained once more against the plastic around them, my whole body tense as I came in Ben's mouth. My hips bucked in his hands, my ass tightening around Xavier's probing finger. The intensity forced my eyes closed, unable to stay open one more second. Slumping back against the seat, my lungs gasped to find air, my heart beating uncontrollably against the wall of my chest. I was spent, unable to move as I let my eyes open again, watching Ben and Xavier kissing, framed sweetly between my splayed thighs.

They stood up, Xavier brandishing a knife from his back pocket. He cut me loose, but I was too tired to get up yet. Stretching my arms over my head, I felt the blood rushing back to my hands, the numbness in my fingers finally dissipating. Slowly, I got dressed, managing to get to my feet, and found myself in Ben and Xavier's arms. They held me up as I regained my strength and came back to life.

'So, Scott, what did you think of the movie?'

Ben couldn't keep the laughter out of his voice, Xavier joining him in a good chuckle.

'Amazing. I can't wait until next year's festival.'

Xavier kissed me on the lips, his hot hands sneaking

under my T-shirt. He sounded equally unconvinced when he spoke.

'So, we've converted you then, Scott?'

'Well, I think I might need some more convincing. How about we go home and watch one of those horrible DVDs you guys have?'

Ben swatted me on the ass as we walked out of the theatre, putting his arms around both of us.

'Great idea. I'll grab some more festival bracelets.'

## Model Me
## by Lynn Lake

Louis gulped, watching as the man came through the door of the classroom and walked up to the front of the class, stepped onto the raised platform.

'This is Guy,' Professor Mansfield said with a slight smile on his face. 'He'll be modelling for us the next three classes – in various poses. You'll all get to know him quite – intimately over that time. And, hopefully,' he added with an arched eyebrow, 'learn to project the human form on to paper with some artistic precision.'

Louis stared at Guy, at the tall man's shoulder-length, glossy black hair, his large, liquid brown eyes, the square, dimpled chin and strong, high-cheekboned face. He still hadn't taken a breath since the man in the white bathrobe had entered the stuffy, third-floor classroom. And now he almost choked, when Professor Mansfield turned to the model and said, 'Guy, if you please.'

The man loosened the sashes at his waist and opened his robe, shrugged it off.

The garment sighed to the floor, the women in the room sighing with it, as the man fully revealed himself. Louis tore his eyes off Guy's face and rolled them down Guy's body.

The model was as beautiful as any Old Master's painting, an original unveiled right there in front of the class. Shoulders broad and buff and bronze, arms hanging loose and long and corded with muscle, chest humped and cleaved, almost as broad as his shoulders, smooth as his arms, studded with twin, tan nipples. His chiselled torso tapered exquisitely down to a narrow wasp waist, from which his legs poured long and caramel-coloured, thighs widened with even more muscle.

Louis licked his cracked, dry lips, as he studied that which all of the women and men (straight and otherwise) were openly gaping unartistically at – the smooth, cut, hooded cock that dangled from the model's groin to awesome effect. The tan member with the moulded crown hung farther down than any flaccid penis had the right to hang, over notably shaven balls.

The stunned silence of the class was shattered by Professor Mansfield clearing his throat and declaring, 'All right, class, you may pick up your charcoal and begin drawing.'

Everyone did, except Louis. He still stared empty-handed and full-blooded at the golden Adonis on stage, casually posed now with one foot slightly ahead of the other, one leg bent, back straight and arms hanging, eyes looking out over the heads of the wannabe artists. Louis explored every shining square inch of the model's frame with his unblinking eyes, focusing more often than not on those petulant, puffy nipples, that monster of a cock even unerect. He couldn't see the man's buttocks, but he could picture them – picture-perfect mounded bronze meaty swells.

'A blank sheet?' Professor Mansfield rumbled close by. 'This isn't an *abstract* art class, young man.'

Louis broke out of his trance. He looked at the professor, grinned nervously, reddened anxiously, applied charcoal to paper happily.

He was a quick draw, and he had the manly model

down in detail in half the time it took the rest of the class. The cock was perhaps even more out of proportion than real life, the nipples flared even more blatantly maybe, but it was still a very good likeness. Louis liked it, a lot, and when Professor Mansfield was otherwise occupied with other budding Rembrandts, he flipped up a couple of sheets on his easel and rapidly went to work on a second rendering of Guy – a representation not just from life, but from fervent imagination as well.

After ten minutes more of feverish drawing, Louis glanced up at his golden idol, and saw that Guy was looking at him, watching him work surreptitiously. The man smiled, and Louis hastily dropped the sheets of paper to cover up his latest creation, his face shading crimson under the model's warm gaze.

The class was soon over. Guy wrapped himself back up in his robe and padded out of the room, to audible groans from some of the women, grunts of relief from some of the guys. The professor and the students exited the classroom as well, leaving Louis behind, all alone – to put some finishing touches on his two compositions. He was planning to hang both sketches in his bathroom that night.

'You really captured me,' someone said from behind, making the talented artist jump.

He spun around, shock sending the stick of charcoal shooting out of his sweaty hand. Guy was standing there, looking at Louis' sketch of himself in his pose for the class, his brown eyes twinkling, big, strong hands clenching the sashes on his robe.

'Uh, th-thanks,' Louis spluttered, even more awed by the man's gorgeousness up close.

Guy displayed his dazzling white teeth in a smile. 'But what was that other picture you were working on? Can I see that one?'

Louis fluttered his long fingers up to his pointed chin, bobbed his bony shoulders. 'Uh, what other picture? There's just the one – for class.'

Guy leant forward, flipped the well-done drawing of himself over, two more pages. Revealing another fully fleshed-out picture – with someone else now up on the dais with Guy, in front of him, gripping his cock, sucking on his nipples.

'You do have an artistic – bent, don't you?' the model commented.

Louis looked at the lewd drawing, at Guy's strikingly handsome face. He shuffled his feet, opened and closed his mouth, waved his hands around.

Guy put him out of his misery, and into pure ecstasy, by pulling the sashes on his robe open again, shrugging the white garment off his bronzed shoulders for a second time. Louis ceased his dance of nervousness and stared at the naked man, the dangling prick that was the absolute model of male lust.

'Something like this, then,' Guy said, gripping Louis' arms and pulling him close, up against his tanned, ripped, heated physique.

Louis just about swooned, his own body temperature skyrocketing, cock leaping in his bohemian black jeans. He was eight inches shorter than the model, so that his mouth was level with the rugged chest, lips in line with those succulent-looking nipples. His hand hung close to that well-hung appendage down below. He could smell the faint musk of the living god, feel the throb and twitch of the powerful muscles, the tender smoothness of the sun-browned skin.

'Like this, and this.' Guy placed one of Louis' hands on his cock, drew Louis' lips onto a nipple.

Louis full-body shuddered, thrilling from tip to toe. He encircled Guy's tremendous organ – barely – with his trembling fingers, gripping the massive tool. It pulsed, thickened, lengthened in his soft, damp palm as he flowered his red lips around the proffered nipple, tasting the delightful rubberiness, the swelling rigidness, the pebble-textured areola.

'That's about what you were trying to portray, isn't it?' Guy said, glancing from the naughty picture to the naughty artist.

Louis bobbed his head slightly, not wanting to break lip contact with that luscious nipple. It was blossoming in his mouth, like Guy's cock was expanding in his hand. He could feel the beat of the man's heart through his tongue and palm. His own heart was racing like a rabbit's, his own nipples buzzing under his black smock, cock bulging his jeans, ballooning with pleasure.

Louis sucked on Guy's nipple. He moved his hand back and forth, stroking Guy's cock. The model of muscular maledom moaned his approval, saying, 'I feel what you're getting at.'

Then he broke away, and scooped up his robe and slipped it back on. Leaving Louis frozen in despair, his lips pouted and cheeks billowing, hand grasping at air.

'Let's see if you can improve on it next class,' Guy said with a wink and a grin.

The next class couldn't come soon enough for Louis, his own frequent coming, as he stared at his drawings and pictured again and again in his mind the encounter they'd engendered, doing nothing to diminish his enthusiasm for his subject.

He was shaking with sheer artistic expression when Guy finally strolled into class, up onto the dais, sat down in the chair Professor Mansfield had placed on the platform. The model looked exactly as before when he disrobed, only sitting now, one arm casually draped over the back of the chair, his head turned to the side in stunning profile, his legs wide apart to reveal the glory of his cock. Louis thought the splendid appendage hung just a little lower, was pumped just a little thicker, thanks to the knowing glance artist and model had exchanged before Guy took the stage.

The class was also swelled by additional members – gawkers who'd come to see the beautiful model everyone in Continuing Ed was talking about. No one was disappointed by what they saw.

'All right, class!' Professor Mansfield shouted above the tumult of appreciative murmuring. 'The male nude – seated. You may now begin drawing.'

Charcoal scraped against paper. Women stared and blushed and tingled, warmly. Men elbowed and pointed and laughed, uneasily. Louis sketched quickly and boldly, ever more confidently.

'Excellent work,' Professor Mansfield remarked.

'I'm, uh, not quite done,' Louis said, grinning shyly.

'Yes, I can see that. Well, keep at it.'

The second sketch was a detailed, wondrously rendered drawing of Guy seated in his chair like a king on his throne, with another man now bowing down on his knees in front, sucking on the model's cock.

'Like this, you mean,' Guy said, drawing up the chair once the classroom had emptied and sitting down again, drawing Louis close and pushing the quivering artist down onto his knees.

'Exactly like this,' Louis breathed, staring at Guy's cock right in front of him, inches away from his burning face. He reached out to grab the semi-erect tool, covet it, worship it.

'Hold on.' Guy intervened, stopping Louis' trembling hand. 'Let me put things in the proper perspective, as you've drawn it.'

Louis watched, his tongue hanging out, as the model's cock swelled on its own, rose up, hood expanding and sniffing at the air, shaft surging thick and long with blood and desire – the desire to be sucked by Louis. He excitedly reached out and wrapped both of his hands around the throbbing, hard shaft, poured his lips over the mushroomed hood, unable to control himself.

Guy grunted and jerked, his pecs jumping, legs clasping the man at his cock in between. Louis swiftly plunged his mouth as far down the wicked dong as he could. He gripped the base, sealed his lips halfway down, letting the member inflate the final few inches inside the warm, wet, velvet-lined cavern of his mouth.

Guy grasped Louis' mouse-brown hair and gently bobbed the man's head up and down in his lap. Louis shook with passion, ablaze with lust, sucking on the model-perfect cock. Its dimensions were the thing of Greek wet dreams. It filled Louis' mouth and part of his throat and all of his soul.

Guy stabilised Louis' head, pumped his hips, fucking the art lover's face. His cock oiled back and forth in between Louis' lips, stroking the man's tongue and mouth, Louis' breath steaming out of his nose and flooding Guy's groin and stomach.

Louis slid a hand up onto Guy's chest, pinched the nipple he'd sucked a week earlier, rolled it. While he slid his other hand down onto Guy's balls, clasping and fondling the man's heavy, shaved sack. Guy's cock glided out to the lips, then plunged back into the mouth deep as it would go, crowding Louis' throat. It pulsed as it pumped, and Louis tasted a sweet, salty drop of precome sprung from the gaping slit.

That's when Guy suddenly drew his hips all the way back, and eased Louis, gasping, away from his groin. 'I can't wait to see your next sketch,' the model said with promise.

The next class exhibit was the "reclining nude male" for the eager students to draw. Professor Mansfield had set up a futon on the dais, and to watching, wide eyes Guy shucked his robe and lay down on his side on the padded piece of furniture. His cock hung down his right thigh, hood pressing into the white fabric of the futon like it had pressed into the back of Louis' throat a week earlier.

The muse-driven artist slashed at his paper in a frenzy, sending charcoal sharding off on either side. He captured the built beauty of the reclining model in mere minutes, as the rest of the class laboured on around him. Oblivious to the others, he flipped the completed drawing over and attacked the next blank sheet of paper with gusto.

He just about jumped out of his skin when he heard Professor Mansfield state, 'Seems you possess quite the fertile imagination, Louis. And the good taste to go along with it.'

The Professor smiled, gazing admiringly at Louis' latest, hottest creation.

Guy smiled, as well, when Louis unveiled the picture to him after class. 'Let's see if we can create life out of art,' he said, taking Louis by the hand.

They climbed up onto the dais, and Guy helped Louis disrobe. The artist's body was thin and pale next to his model's, but fully animated where it counted – between the legs. Louis' cock jutted out long and hard and pink and purple-capped from his loins.

Guy took a tube out of a pocket of his robe before he removed the garment. Then he stretched out on his side on the futon as during class, except now his cock was as hard as Louis', stroked slick with the lube from the tube.

Louis settled down on his side in front of Guy, replicating the erotic picture he'd drawn. He jerked when he felt Guy's slippery fingers slide in between his quivering buttocks, moaned when the fingers scrubbed up and down, all around his asshole.

'Shall I put the finishing touch on your masterpiece?' Guy breathed in Louis' ear.

Louis nodded, gripping the edge of the futon, feeling the heat of the model's body so close, the heft of the man's cockhead up against his pucker. Guy kissed Louis' neck, pressing forward with his cock, squishing the knob into Louis' starfish. He popped ass ring, plunged chute, ploughing his huge tool deep into the heated, gripping confines of Louis' anus.

Louis shook out of control, his ass swelled with Guy's cock inside, his body shimmering with electric sensation.

Guy gripped Louis' shoulder with one strong hand, coiled his other muscular arm around the quivering man's neck, and pumped his hips, fucking Louis' ass. He started slow, the futon creaking, Louis gasping, cock sluicing sure and sensual. Then he upped the tempo, churning his hips, ramming Louis' butt, sawing the man's chute. The futon scraped to the rocking motion, Louis moaning, Guy breathing hard, thighs slapping against buttocks, cock stretching and stuffing anus.

It went on like that for a blistering minute or so. Before shifting to frenzy level, Guy powerfully pistoning his hips, pile-driving Louis' ass with his hammering cock. Louis almost lost consciousness under the anal onslaught, Guy's arm crushing his neck, cock splitting his bum, banging him to and fro. He desperately grabbed his own flapping cock, and stroked, once.

That was all it took under the feverish, superheated circumstances. Louis bleated joy, jetted ecstasy. Just as Guy slammed as deep as he could and then shuddered, sprayed, splashing Louis' bowels with searing semen.

Louis' clenching ass muscles clamped down on Guy's shunting, pumping cock, the artist convulsing with orgasm. The model brushed Louis' hand away from his spouting cock and gripped and ripped it himself, sending Louis into further spasms of white-hot delight. Until both men were drained of all artistic and sexual expression.

They rented a loft together, artist and model. Louis set up a studio on the upper floor, and Guy posed for him, both professionally and personally.

It was a picture-perfect relationship. Up until the day Guy was idly looking through Louis' latest sketches, as Louis took a shower after another one of his classes, and the model found, buried amidst the drawings of fruit and flowers, an explicit sketch of a well-hung figure bent over a couch while another figure fucked him in the ass. The man with his cock buried anally bore a striking resemblance to the artist. While the man getting reamed was built along Guy's lines, only his skin was shaded in much, much darker.

Guy let out a growl, picked up a stick of charcoal and stomped down the stairs to the bathroom, where Louis was happily painting his prick with a sudsy hand in the hot spray of the shower, mentally canvassing the model he'd just met in class.

## Taking the Bait
### by P.A. Friday

You can see him ahead of you in the dark back street, walking slowly and giving a quick look back over his shoulder every now and again. He knows you are there; he has been waiting for you. For days now, as you leave work, he has been there – baiting you, waiting for you to give in. No matter what time it is when you leave (a glance at your watch tells you it is not quite 11 p.m.), he is always there. This time, he will believe you have taken his bait – and to an extent he is right. You will give him what he wants. But you will punish him a little for his temerity first.

You catch him up. You push him against the wall of the building, arms forced above his head by your hands, one thigh thrust between his legs. He is in your power. He is perhaps taller than you, a fraction; but you are broader, heavier. You could take him on any time and win. But it is another sort of taking you have in mind tonight.

'Waiting for someone?' you ask.

He is pretty. Oh, he is pretty. He looks across at you with a faint, cocky smile on his face.

'Why would you think that?' he says.

Why indeed. 'I think you were waiting for me.'

'Maybe.'

'I think you want me to fuck you.'

His control breaks for the first time, a shudder of

desire running through him. You think, passingly, how strange it seems to you that such a pretty young man wants you so much.

'Maybe,' he whispers again.

You lean in towards him, and the backs of his hands scrape against the bricks. Then … Oh no, that is not a kiss; it is a mark of possession. He struggles against you – but not to get away. Instead, he rubs himself up against your leg, his erection hard against your thigh. His breathing quickens. But this is too far too fast. You are not going to allow him to choose the manner of his taking. You move back, just a step. He makes a small noise of protest in his throat, which cuts off as you drop one hand to his belt, holding his wrists firmly in the other. He thinks he has you now – that you are going to do anything, everything he wants. He doesn't know you so very well yet. He will learn. You unfasten the buckle of his belt, and slide it out of its moorings so that the leather lies against your palm. Your gaze is locked with his.

'Take your shirt off,' you tell him.

He is wise enough to be obedient. You let go of his hands and they drop to the hem of his white T-shirt, and he pulls it over his head and off. He is more muscular than you thought at first; there is a sprinkling of dark hairs on his chest. You allow yourself to look for as long as you choose, then hold out your hand for the T-shirt. He gives it up, and you throw it on the ground, discarded. It has served its purpose; it is irrelevant from now on. Feeding the belt through its buckle again, you slip the loop over his head and buckle it on the closest hole. People have always wondered why you have a hole bored in your belt so far round; no man, surely, could be that thin. But it is not made for encompassing a waist.

He stills suddenly, perhaps realising for the first time

that he has underestimated you. You jerk your head, and with a tug of the belt make him understand that he is to follow you. You hold the end of the belt in your hand like a lead.

You know where you are headed. You know precisely where you want to go. He told you, once, where he lived. Not so far from here, though you will have to walk through a couple of more populated streets to get there. If he wants you, he's going to have to prove it, walking behind you on his lead, naked from the waist up. You smile at the image, turning your head to admire your docile young man, following obediently wherever you go. He holds his head high, and meets your eye as you look round. He knows this is a test, and he is passing it. Oh, he is passing it.

As you walk down Friar's Lane, you see your first strangers – and they see you. You wonder what they think is going on. He shows the first sign of discomfort, attempting to lengthen his stride in order to catch you up. You halt.

'Oh no,' you chastise him. 'That is not your decision to make.'

You wonder whether he will be prepared to accept this, or whether he will walk away. You try and tell yourself you don't care which he chooses, but you know it is a lie. You want him, this pretty boy – but you want him on your own terms. It is up to him to accept or refuse. He bows his head a little in submission.

You start walking again, and he follows. A few more people stop and look; a couple make drunken comments. Neither you nor he takes any notice. You are locked in your own world. The streets are deserted again as you reach his road. It is a quiet street with apartments rising up on either side of the road, and it's mostly inhabited by well-off single guys – like him. It's unlikely that anyone will pass this way at this time of night, but there's still a chance that someone may come at any moment. If he wants you, he will have to risk showing the whole street what he is, what he likes to do. If he wants you, he will play by your rules. He deserves this for the shameless play he's made for you, thinking he could twist you round his little finger. He picked the wrong guy to play games with. You know games he's never even thought of; you wrote the rules – and then broke them all in turn – of this particular sort of game. You unbuckle the belt from his neck and look hard at him.

There is tension running through him. He is fizzing like shaken champagne.

'Kids who look for trouble tend to find it,' you say softly. You run a finger down his chest. 'Are you looking for trouble?'

He doesn't speak. You kiss him again, marking your conquest, then take his ear between your teeth for a second, biting a just little harder than will have been comfortable.

'I said,' you repeat, 'are you looking for trouble?'

His breath hisses through his lips. 'Yes,' he says.

Concise and to the point. 'Good,' you say. 'Kiss me.'

He puts warm lips against your own, gentle to contrast with your own rougher approach. You expected that, though, just as you guessed what else he would try. He wraps his arms around your neck and presses close. Despite his recent humiliating walk, he is still hard. He is trying to seduce you, distract you. You will allow him to play off his tricks for a while; it is amusing to see what he does. He is good too; his is not the only hard, erect cock. But you are never going to allow him to succeed. This is *your* show, not his. He hooks one of his legs around you, as ivy might cast its tendrils around an oak tree. You are hard and unmoving as oak; he as tricksy as ivy. He still thinks he has a chance of control – the unending optimism of youth. He rubs against you, nestling as close as he can to your body. The feeling is pleasant – more than pleasant; there is a temptation to give in, to allow this young man to do what he wants. But, almost despite yourself, you are unable to let go like that.

With your hands around his waist you lift him away from you. He is heavier than you might once have expected, but after seeing his muscular physique when he took off his shirt, you are not altogether surprised.

'We do things my way,' you say huskily.

'Yes.'

A surprise: his response is fervent and eager. You had anticipated, perhaps, an edge of disappointment from him at not getting his own way. He looks like a young man who is very used to getting his own way. Perhaps he is bored of that; you present a different challenge. Perhaps that was always what he saw in you, why the pretty boy was making moves on the older, more rugged man. Perhaps he has always wanted to be dominated. It is a pleasing conceit, but now is not the moment for it. You can consider his motivation later; at the moment, it is his body you wish to consider.

'On your knees.'

He drops to the ground. He is more than pretty; kneeling at your feet he is beautiful. You wrench your jeans undone, and he takes the hint, shuffling forward and raising a greedy mouth to your cock. His hands are cold as he pulls your cock free, but the warmth of his mouth makes up for that. He flicks his tongue against the head, and you take a sudden heavy breath at the sensation. He is good – practised. You wonder for a second where he has garnered his experience before you cease to care as he continues his ministrations. He could suck you to completion, easily, but you don't want that. You want to come when you're deep in his arse; you want to thrust inside him so hard against his prostate he sees stars. You want to have him begging before you reach your peak. You move away, and he stays on his knees.

'Please,' he says.

He is flushed and hot, despite the cold evening air. No one has come past, but you suspect he wouldn't give a damn if the entire street was watching. Suddenly it is you who cares. You want to keep this pretty boy to yourself.

'Get up,' you order. He obeys, and you kiss him, tasting yourself on his mouth. 'Good boy.' You smile a little. 'Do you want me to fuck you now?'

He still meets your gaze with that fearless, shameless look. 'You know I do.'

You lick a path up his neck to his ear. 'Then ask me nicely,' you whisper.

'Please,' he says again. 'Fuck me, please.' His control slips a little. 'God, do what you want with me,' he adds, his voice unsteady.

He could have said nothing which would please you more. You knew that he would be waiting for you tonight, and you made your preparations in advance. You unbutton his flies and push his trousers and pants down. His cock springs free and you grasp it for a second, stroking it through your fingers.

'Turn round.'

He bites his lip a second; you can see he wants you to touch him again, more – or, if you will not, to touch himself. He's learnt by now that you won't allow that, and pride won't let him ask.

'Soon,' you promise.

It is unusual for you to give out promises; you wonder whether the boy has not won after all, but it hardly matters now, as he turns away and braces himself against the wall. You dig in your pocket for the lube you put there, and squeeze some onto your fingers. As you prep him, you reach your other hand around and hold his erection hard in your palm. He groans, thrusting his hips back against your fingers and then forward, driving his cock harder into your left hand. So eager.

'Are you ready for me?' you ask.

He gives a laugh which is half a groan. 'Yeah.'

The condom slides over your erect cock with ease, and you place the head at his entrance.

'Sure?' you ask, making him wait for it.

'Please,' he says again, his voice almost a whine.

You'd thought, when considering it, that you'd take him hard from the start – further punishment for his cocksure belief that he could snap his fingers and you'd come running. But now, looking down at his glorious arse, feeling the heat of his cock – remembering the way he had sounded as he said "do what you want with me" – you slide into him with rare gentleness. His forehead drops forward against the wall as you move deeper inside him, feeling the muscle give way under your pressure.

'Do you like that?' you ask, teasing yourself and him with your self-control.

'Yes. God. Please.'

He rocks his hips, but you bite into the soft flesh of his shoulder.

'Wait.'

His fingernails scrape against the wall as he tries to obey your order. And now even you cannot wait any longer. Slowly at first, then faster, you move inside him, your fingers simulating the movement on his cock. He is all hitched breathing and desire; a potent mixture. Did you think he would be good? You never thought he'd be this good. You increase the motion, angling yourself so you hit that one spot inside him which will send him over the edge. The breaths have become moans; cries which he can't suppress. There is sweat beading on his neck; you swipe your tongue across it, tasting him.

'Please,' he cries, and that final word brings you both to your climax; you feel his come across your fingers as you pulse inside him.

Afterwards, you stay for a moment, locked into position: your head against his shoulder, his head against the wall. It takes some time for your breathing to return to normal; you can feel the thump of his heartbeat through his body. At last you pull out, and he sighs and turns to face you once more.

'Did you find what you were looking for?' you ask.

His cocky smile is back again. 'Yes,' he says, his tone wicked. 'Did you?'

He knows you won't answer, but knows too what the answer is.

Yes.

# Kissing the Gunner's Daughter
## by Beverly Langland

I huddled closer to the inn wall, peering down the long dark wharf toward the harbour mouth. I could barely make out the masts of the *Mediator* as she slipped silently into the distance. Only the intermittent glow of her cabin lights broke the blacker distance seaward. Night was drawing in and I had not yet taken enough money to buy even a mouldy crust. On this bleak night the inn was barely half-full and a glance inside confirmed my suspicion that I had already propositioned most of those inside. Charity was hard to find in this part of the world. I was about to haul anchor when I spotted an old sailor limping towards the inn. He had but one foot, the other lopped away. I intercepted him before he could circumnavigate my position. I held out my palm, for I am a wretched creature, forced by circumstance to beg for my supper. 'Kind sir, would you spare a boy, down on his luck, the price of a meal?'

The seafarer, perhaps alone in an unfamiliar port, looked kindly on me. 'What's your name, laddie?'

'George, sir. George Ludlow.'

'So, Master Ludlow, how come ye to this situation?'

'Sir, my story is long.'

The old man looked into my eyes and I saw a spark of decency in his. 'Then come into the inn and sup with me. Ye can tell me your tale over a bowl of hot mutton stew.'

It was an offer I could not ignore. We moved into the warmth of the inn, whence the old sailor not only bought me supper, but also spared a few extra coppers for a jug of ale. 'So now, laddie, how come ye to Antigua?'

I looked into his kindly face and wondered if I could tell him the truth of my ordeal. He smiled a crooked smile, showing two gold teeth in an otherwise remarkable collection for a man of his age. 'Sir,' I said, 'I am a fugitive from His Majesty's navy. I was put ashore in disgrace at St John's Road.'

In truth, my tale was unremarkable. I was sufficiently educated to become a midshipman on HMS *Mediator* after a few months of training. Life on board ship was harsh, harsher than my father led me to believe, and the rotten food, the terrors of combat, and the strict discipline enforced by Captain Hamilton and his boatswain, Mr Tuttle, quickly eclipsed the romance instilled by my father's readings of the sea. I told the old seadog all this, but it was nothing he didn't know already. He was more interested in the details of my downfall, and he told me as much. He said his name was McGuire, but I should call him captain. He was in charge of a clipper, making the rounds of the Main and the Carribee before heading back to Boston. The captain stuffed tobacco into a long clay pipe as he eyed me, waiting for my story.

'Well sir, youth often runs wild, and I am no different. The captain and his lady were in his cabin, I was on first watch, a little bored, and curious of the laughter and high-pitched squeals coming from below. I had the deck, so I strolled aft, drawing closer to the noise, only to find I had ventured too far. In his haste to please the lady, the captain had failed to draw his curtains, and through the window, I saw ... Well, let me say the captain had intimately entwined with his lady. I should have turned

42

away immediately, but my curiosity got the better of me. I'm afraid that I lingered too long and the captain spied me. I hurried back to my post, but of course it was already too late.

'Nothing was said until the following morning, when the captain sent for me. My indiscretion had the captain riled and he threatened me with a Court Martial. However, as it was my first offence since boarding the *Mediator*, the surgeon persuaded the captain to change his mind. So, instead, the captain ordered that I receive 21 lashes, the punishment to take place on deck in front of the crew as a deterrent to other miscreants. If needs be, the captain said, young gentlemen aboard his ship had to be whipped into shape, and it was clear that I was to take a measure of his stern discipline.

'Prior to my flogging I had to make my own pussy, a cut-down cat with only five tails, binding the whipcord lengths to the handle. By regulation, the flogging of all midshipmen takes place on the bare posterior. Sir, I cannot describe the ignominy I felt when Mr Tuttle, a dark, grim-faced man, pulled my breeches down around my ankles to reveal my bottom and much else besides. He tied me in a bending position to a field gun moved into the centre of the deck, my body lying lengthways along the barrel, with my wrists tied together underneath so that I embraced the barrel, my abdomen resting on a folded hammock.'

'Kissing the gunner's daughter,' the captain chimed in.

'Aye, captain, some folk call it so. Mr Tuttle gave me a piece of hide to bite on before he started. He delivered each stroke slow and deliberate. The boatswain paused between lashes to ensure that I fully experienced the pain, and because the tails of the pussy often became entwined and required separating. Mr Tuttle offered me water after

11 strokes, which I took gladly, wishing to delay the rest of the beating. After the 21st and final stroke, Mr Tuttle untied me from the gun barrel and I stood to face the other young gentlemen and the rest of the crew who had been mustered to witness my punishment. I quickly pulled up my breeches, trying to hide an errant erection, which had come unbidden. I turned to Captain Hamilton, and thanked him. A glass was over the captain's arm and a wry grimace on his lips. Then the first mate made a short and succinct address and dismissed the crew.

'The ship's surgeon, Dr Lyle, witnessed the beating, as he was required by regulation to attend, and afterwards he walked me to his cabin, giving me encouragement and telling me to be brave. Once in his cabin the surgeon wanted to examine me, so I had to remove my breeches once more. There was only superficial bleeding, the surgeon said, and little permanent damage, though my buttocks felt like they were on fire. Dr Lyle said he had a soothing balm that would help. He bid me lie on the table while he applied the unction. His hands were firm, and the balm cold, drawing the fire in my flesh to the surface. All the while, he offered his reassuring words.

'Yet the surgeon's kindness was conditional. He wanted something in return that he said only a young man of my particular nature could provide.' I paused at this point, wondering how much of my story I should reveal to this stranger, for truth was I felt I had been complicit in my own undoing.

'What did the surgeon want, laddie?'

'Please understand, captain, that estranged from my hitherto genteel life and feeling brutalised by the flogging, I was in much need of comfort. The doctor's eyes promised this and much more, and I in my innocence fell afoul of him. While I was still lying on the surgeon's table, he turned me onto my side to gain access to my cock. Now, sir, despite the agonising pain of the flogging I must confess that the beating had turned my manhood rigid, a fact Dr Lyle could not fail to notice. I prayed that my cock would return to its normal flaccid condition, but the application of the soothing balm, and the surgeon's strong hands on my buttocks, fuelled my cock with fresh blood. I was deeply embarrassed, but the surgeon told me not to worry. My aroused state, he said, was common in young midshipmen following a public flogging.

'I was much relieved by his words. However, my cock still poked into the air, and Dr Lyle said he should do something to relieve my discomfort before my condition caused permanent injury. The surgeon grasped my cock in his large hand, his smooth palms showing that he had never done a day's hard work. If my manhood had been rigid before, it immediately turned to granite at his manly touch. The surgeon held my cock with more confidence than I ever had, and started to pump me with vigour. I wasn't sure that milking me was strictly necessary, but the surgeon gave me his assurance that it would greatly aid my recovery. "Shouldn't I do it?" I asked, for my fellow midshipmen and I were already acquainted with this form of relief. As you may know, sir, accommodation aboard His Majesty's frigates is greatly restricted, and privacy is not a consideration, so the midshipmen had an unwritten pact to close our minds to the quiet night-time fumblings of our fellows.

'I had to grit my teeth against the pleasurable contact of the surgeon's hand. After a time a little lubricant escaped, at which point the surgeon smeared my liquid over my cock with his fingers. "Now … That's more like it," he said, as I started to moan. In spite of my misgivings, I was enjoying the strength of his hand wrapped around my cock. There is little human contact on board ship, so the closeness of Dr Lyle was a novelty. It seemed that the surgeon was experienced at extracting pleasure, for he soon had me spurting into a bowl he had placed on the table. We looked at each other, I wide-eyed and feeling flushed in the face, but his eyes turned dark. The surgeon smiled in his grim fashion, his lips thin like an old, pale scar as he helped me off the table.

'Dr Lyle pushed my slight weight to the deck before fumbling with his breeches and freeing his erection. I shook my head back and forth, trying to escape Dr Lyle's angry-looking cock. "I do not want this doctor, I do not wa –" My objection was cut off as the surgeon, perhaps tired of playing with me, reached forward and yanked me by my hair, pulling so hard that I yelped in pain. He brought my head closer to his member, which he then rubbed over my face. I looked to him for guidance, but, "Suck my cock," is all he said.

'As I opened my mouth, Dr Lyle pushed himself into my warm, wet orifice, moving before I had time to react. I almost gagged as he pushed forward. My breath burned harshly in my throat, as with one hand he held the back of my head, while with the other he guided his member in and out of my mouth. It didn't feel right that he should be stabbing my face with his cock, yet I was surprised how quickly I grew accustomed to the feeling. Finally, certain that I did not intend to bite, the surgeon used both his hands to hold my head firmly in place. With his breeches bunched around his ankles, he used my mouth to achieve his own gratification.

'Sir, I fear to describe what happened next, but as a man of the world perhaps I will not shock. The grunts of Dr Lyle's passion, mixed with slurping noises and my soft whimpers of protest, filled the surgeon's cabin. It was pointless to fight, for Dr Lyle had the captain's favour, and it would be his word against mine. Gasping, the surgeon threw his head back and moaned in ecstasy. Suddenly, he let out a low grunt, as though someone had punched him in the stomach, before collapsing back against the cabin wall with the sated sigh of a pleased lover. Dr Lyle left me kneeling on the deck with my mouth full, his warm seed oozing from the side of my mouth. I looked about me for somewhere to spit, but the bowl had gone. The surgeon laughed and told me to swallow. He looked more like a fierce, bold-eyed rascal than a benefactor. I swallowed. I remember still the bitter tang in my mouth, and the unendurable atrocity Dr Lyle had forced me to perform.

'It was in Portsmouth that I informed my father of the flogging. This provoked Father to write an anguished letter to the captain, complaining of my ill-treatment. The captain replied that he had caught me in the act of watching through his cabin window, and he had had the boatswain inflict the punishment in the usual way. Dissatisfied with the captain's reply, Father then wrote to the Admiralty, but they gave him short shrift. At my father's insistence, I returned to the *Mediator* filled with dread. From the moment of my boarding, Captain Hamilton and the boatswain paid particular attention to my conduct and my performance. Punishments were open to the caprice of the captain. Whenever he found me slacking, the boatswain set about me with the cane. Six strokes applied to the hands was authorised but, because it impaired my ability to climb the rigging, the captain authorised posterior chastisement. After each beating I was required to visit the surgeon on the captain's orders.'

'Dr Lyle picked on me unmercifully. After my treatments – usually the application of the pungent balm made from whale lard – the surgeon *expressed* my seed into the porcelain bowl, for my own benefaction, he said. Afterwards I had to give thanks by kneeling on the cabin floor to take him into my mouth. I was always obliged to swallow the evidence of the dirty deed and sworn to secrecy. The surgeon had no need to worry. There was no one to tell, no one who would believe me at any rate. To my knowledge, I was the only midshipman treated in this appalling and disgraceful manner. I believe, sir, there is something about me which encourages bad behaviour in others, something in my look, perhaps. I weathered the punishments well enough and, for a time, there was a lull, but the kind of lull that fetched round more wind, and the surgeon's demands of me grew. Sir, he had a dark soul!

'I thought my ordeal would never end, but I garnered courage and finally challenged Dr Lyle, refusing to kowtow in front of him. The blaggard did not back off with grace, but falsely accused me of stealing. His Majesty's navy takes such a crime seriously. I believe the captain took this opportunity to rid himself of me. To his way of thinking, I had never fitted with his manner of command and had caused him sorrow from the day I boarded. He ordered another flogging in front of the crew, and so I found myself strapped to the field gun for a second time. I was to receive thirty lashes! The boatswain, never one to hold back, put all his effort into my punishment.

'Afterwards, there was no visit to the surgeon. I was simply put ashore, with no money and no friends, to make my own way home. So, sir, we come to the present. You have the truth, and my purpose.'

'Well, laddie. That is some adventure,' the captain said, as I finished the rest of my draught. We talked some more about life at sea, and sailing in general and I got the impression the captain was testing me on my knowledge. I was only a midshipman, but I had spent two years at sea and I hoped I gave a good account of myself. The captain had stuck to the sea most of his life. He had done things; he had fought the redskins in Canada and the English on Hudson Bay and the Spanish in Brazil, and he had tales to tell. Then he made me a proposition. 'Here's the way of it,' he said as he puffed at the tobacco. 'I've lost my cabin boy to the fever and I am in need of a replacement.'

'A cabin boy?'

'Aye. I can't offer ye more. Perhaps when we change crew in Boston.'

I replied that I would sleep on his offer.

'Then ye have a place to sleep?' I told him that I knew of a stable not far from the inn, where the stable hand turned a blind eye to the occupation of an empty stall.

'A stable? I will not bear you sleeping in a stable.'

I replied that without means I had no choice.

The captain thought for a moment, rubbing his chin through his beard. We were alone before the embers of the fire, and his eyes were amber reflections. 'I will foot the bill should ye wish to occupy the cot in my room.'

Again, I was not in a position to refuse, not if I wanted to sleep in a comfortable cot for the night, and I didn't want to lose sight of the captain should I decide to take up on his offer and go back to sea. He might well change his mind over the proposal. We retired to his room and I lit candles. The room was homely, but afforded far greater comfort than I had seen for many months. There was a washbasin and a jug of clean water. At the captain's insistence, I washed first, stripping to the waist. The captain stood close behind me and examined the stripes on my lower back, his rough fingers surprisingly gentle. He made no comment; he simply traced the lines of the scars to the edge of my breeches. Then, still not speaking he reached about my waist to untie the cord and eased my breeches over my buttocks.

I closed my eyes as he continued his silent exploration, getting ever closer to the crack of my bottom. Yet the captain surprised me, changing the path of his journey until he had reached the root of my manhood. He grabbed hold of my flaccid cock and squeezed, forcing life into my cock, until it was bulging with blood and vitality. He pumped me and I thought that this would be the price of his hospitality. The captain had other thoughts. He moved his hands back to the crease in my bottom, digging his fingers into the soft flesh and spreading my buttocks so that he could spit on my anus. So *this* was to be his prize. I didn't flinch. A man with no means and little hope of employment needed a benefactor. However, I admit that I would never again look unfavourably on the whores in Portsmouth, should I ever return home.

The captain ran his fingers around my hole and rubbed in his spittle. As my anus became slick, he started pushing his fingers forward, trying to get in. I was not hard to enter, but I had neglected to tell the captain that he was not exploring virgin territory. Slowly, one of his fingers slipped inside and he moved it around carefully, as if exploring the possibility of venturing further. His gentle ministrations almost made me spill my seed. After a few minutes, my bowels started to loosen to the captain's satisfaction and he worked in a second stubby finger. Even though my anus had opened, it was still tight, as Dr Lyle took great pleasure in telling me, and I was going to have a hard time to keep from crying out when the old seaman eventually sank his cock inside me; for surely the purpose of his close scrutiny was now plain. Finally, his exploration complete, the captain pulled out his fingers from their warm, soft haven.

'You perhaps omitted something from your tale, young George.' The captain slipped a thick finger back into my anus, and I released an involuntary groan of pleasure. 'Perhaps the surgeon introduced you to the dark pleasures of buggery. Did he bend you over his table as I bend ye now? Did he push his turgid cock deep into your rectum, nudging his way ever deeper into your bowels until ye felt as if ye sat upon the mast?'

I kept my silence. I could not tell for fear of retribution, for sodomy is a capital offence. 'Well, laddie?' The captain slapped my buttocks hard, then hard again, the sting lingering while he awaited my reply. He took hold of my arm and twisted it high up my back.

'Yes,' I shouted, 'yes! To my lasting shame, sir, Dr Lyle forced himself on me.'

The old seaman did not seem to care for the law, for his cock was out of his breeches, as hard as a rod of iron and poking against my buttocks. 'Your secret is safe with me laddie. Who cares about such things at the edge of the world? Did the surgeon hurt you?'

'Yes, captain.' This was the truth. I had quickly discovered that the cunning surgeon paid little heed of my welfare. I wasn't certain the captain did either, for as I spoke he was pressing his cock between my sore bottom cheeks, trying to find the opening to my anus. He rubbed his cock up and down my crack, pausing every time he passed over my puckered hole. I spread my legs a little more, bracing myself. I wanted the captain in me for a reason. I wanted to gain his good grace and this seemed the obvious way. I felt him penetrate my anus and I gasped with the size of the captain's member filling me. He said nothing, just kept pressing his cock deeper. As his cock filled me, I couldn't help but groan. The captain pulled back a little and moved back in, allowing me time to get used to his size. He was breathing rapidly now and gulping for air as his moans joined mine.

The captain took his time, fucking me slowly, the full length of his cock moving in and out of me. I admit my moans soon turned into whimpers as he started fucking me in earnest. My lust was consuming me and he started pounding harder, as if he was trying to get his whole body inside. His hips made a slapping sound when they hit my muscled buttocks. I know little of human anatomy, but the captain's cock nudged something inside me and my own cock, which had gone soft when he first started fucking me, began to fill and swell. The old seaman's cock kept hitting the same spot and my whimpering increased. As he fucked ever faster, I grabbed my member and started pounding, shooting my seed into the air moments later when the captain pushed his cock into me as far as he could and held steady. He filled me with his hot semen. My buttocks tightened and I let out a final strangled groan when I forced out the last drops of my seed.

As my ecstasy ebbed, my body went slack in the captain's arms. 'Steady lad,' he said, 'steady.' He pulled himself out of me and eased me gently to the floor, his errant seed seeping down my leg to join my own, crudely wasted. We stared at each other in silence, the captain's purple face a sign of his exertion and my own skin blotched with hot, red patches, though none as hot as the cheeks of my bottom. The captain took a swig of water and wiped his brow. 'We will never speak of this again, do ye hear!'

'No, captain … I mean, yes, captain.'

'So, what think you of my offer? Are ye with me to the Americas?'

'Aye, captain. I'm your man.'

'Then it's settled.' The old seadog smiled through his grisly beard, then pointed to the floor. 'Ye can make a start by cleaning up that mess.'

I did what the captain bid while he undressed. Deep scars crisscrossed all of his body. He washed and got into his bed. I made to join him, but he held up his hand, stopping me. 'Hold on laddie, the cot's for you.'

My disappointment must have showed for he asked, 'What pains you?'

'I am in need of a little comfort,' I replied.

'Comfort, is it?' His frown faded, replaced by that crooked smile of his, his gold teeth glinting in the candlelight. Then he pulled back the blanket. 'Not one word of this kindness or my crew will think me soft.'

I slipped into the bed and, as I curled next to the captain, I felt his cock twitch. I reached out to discover the beast growing erect in my palm. 'Not soft, captain,' I said. 'Never soft.'

'Then I hope ye will continue to be my guest until I sail to Boston next week. It would be best, I think.'

# Hiding Out in His Sauna
## by Richard Hiscock

Finally, the place was quiet. I'd been on reception since early morning. There was a four-day conference being held at our hotel. Some sort of romance writers' convention. Nearly all were women and I can tell you they varied in age, size, and looks. There were only eight men among them and a couple were really cute.

The last group arrived at about six. Dinner and speeches were from eight until eleven so I knew I could relax between those hours and leave the work to the staff. This was a family business and we all bogged in to help.

After having my own dinner my brother took over so I could work out in the gym. I never missed a day; keeping fit was one of my main proprieties. I like being toned; in my line of work it always pays to look your best and sometimes if I'm lucky I get to score with the odd lonely businessman who's been on the road for a while. It's a perk and I love it. No strings attached.

As I pumped iron my mind began to wonder. It had been quite a while since I'd had any sort of sex apart from masturbation. The last encounter had been so quick it had left me feeling frustrated. The guy had come on to me when I'd taken him some clean towels. He opened the door naked, his lower half hidden. He asked me to come in on the pretence of checking the lock on the bathroom door; said the handle was loose.

He'd filled the spa bath and it was swirling as the jets pumped out water.

'Sorry but I was just about to jump in,' he said, explaining away his nakedness.

He knew I was coming up to the room so he didn't have to be nude. I had the feeling he was gay and by the hardness of his cock I thought he might be looking for some action. I checked the lock, kneeling on the floor with my spanner, which I'd fortunately had in my back pocket.

He was close to me and as I turned to tell him it was OK he just thrust his cock at my face. I couldn't help myself. I grabbed it and swallowed it down. He stood there, pelvis tilted, thrusting in and out while I marvelled at my luck. His cock grew enormously, almost to the point of choking me. A few more thrusts and he was coming in my mouth.

He collapsed against the wall, trying to regain his breath.

'Turn around,' I demanded, my cock now out of my trousers, ready for action.

He did as I asked, leaning on the sink. I pulled him back by the hips so he was bending over further and ran my hand over his cheeks. He sighed as I ran my tongue down the crack of his arse, slathering his puckered hole with saliva.

Prying open his cheeks I eyed his hole, waxed and hair free. It looked so inviting. I couldn't wait to sink my cock in and grabbed my knob, guiding it towards him. He wiggled his bum and my knob slipped in a fraction. His sphincter tightened, but a quick slap on his rump and he relaxed, allowing the knob to slip in further.

Once the knob was in the rest followed easily. I was just beginning to get my rhythm when my fucking phone rang. I ignored it but it rang again, spoiling the moment. He peered back at me from over his shoulder.

'You'd better get that or they might come looking for you,' he said with a laugh.

'What?' I barked into the phone, cock still buried in the guy's arse.

'The heating system has blown a fuse. We don't have any hot water for rooms five to ten,' my brother said. 'You'd better hurry up and fix it.'

I snapped the phone closed and pumped for all I was worth, coming all too quickly. It hadn't been how I wanted it but what could I do?

'Why don't you come back later and hop in the spa with me?' the guy said.

'I'll call you if I have time.' And with that I was gone, running to get the job done.

Unfortunately it took me hours to fix the problem, and then there were other chores to attend to so I never got to have a really good session with him, and even though I'd come it wasn't how I'd wanted it.

So now, after a gruelling gym session I was debating whether to take a swim or just hit the sauna. When you had a crowd in there was always something going wrong and tonight might be one of those nights. I knew I didn't have time for both, so I decided on the latter. I rested in the warmth after just having splashed the coals with icy cold water, the room so steamy I couldn't even see a few inches in front of me.

I was still thinking about that encounter, and how I'd have liked something more satisfying, when a gush of cool air alerted me to the fact that someone had entered. I was annoyed as I really wanted this time to be my own until I heard voices. Men's voices. Intrigued, I kept quiet and waited for the fog to lift to see who was there.

'Oh Mark, thank goodness we're finally alone,' one of them said.

'I know; I've been dying to get my hands on you ever since you arrived.'

'It feels like years since the last time.'

'Yeah, these things don't come around often enough.'

'God, you feel good.'

'Hey,' the one who was called Mark said, 'don't do that. What if someone comes in?'

'Relax, no one will, the place is deserted. They're all listening to Miss High and Mighty giving her lecture on how she got published. Anyway, I can barely see your cock but, God, your balls feel good.'

'Hey, not so hard.' He laughed.

'Sorry, I've missed you, that's all.'

I could feel my cock begin to grow as my interest piqued. They didn't know I was there. I wondered how far they'd go and, more importantly, how long before the steam dwindled and they realised I was there.

'Your cock feels even better.' Mark laughed, a deep growl in his chest.

I gulped. Fuck. These two guys were going to get it on together, right here in the sauna, only a few feet away from me. I was sitting up high in the corner. I wondered how long they'd be able to stand the heat and I was hoping they'd love it because as soon as it began to clear I'd have a bird's eye view of the two of them and if they didn't look up – well, here's hoping.

I hoped they were good-looking, youngish and well-built, the two cute romance writers I'd seen earlier.

'Get these towels underneath you on the seat so you don't hurt your back.'

'You're always so thoughtful,' Mark said.

I still couldn't make them out, but their whispering

turned to moaning and I wondered if I should sneak down a step lower in the hope of seeing more of them.

'God, your cock's great,' the other one said.

'Oh fuck, your mouth, I've missed you so much,' Mark said. 'I'm dying for a good slamming.'

'Fuck me too. I've been so lonely and not being able to confide in anyone back home has made life so difficult.'

'Well, people can be so judgmental,' Mark said. 'At least here we're all in the same boat.'

'What, those new guys too?' he mumbled, his mouth obviously full of Mark's cock.

'Yep, one tried to hit on me last night.'

'What?'

'Don't worry, nothing happened. Get your mouth back on my cock.'

'So, you're not interested in a threesome?'

'Why, are you?'

'I don't know, I haven't really thought about it.'

'Oh yes, you have. Your cock's like a fucking iron rod, you've thought about it all right.'

'Maybe just a little when I'm all alone.' He laughed.

Well now, maybe this might turn out to be beneficial for all of us, I thought. Would I dare join them if the opportunity arose, so to speak?

At last the steam began to dissipate and I saw that they were in the 69 position, one on top with his bum wiggling back, his puckered hole beckoning me while his friend sucked and slurped away.

I slipped out of my bathers and sat naked on the bench, pulling at my cock, watching them and wondering if I should approach them or not. It had been quite a while for me too; I hadn't been in a serious relationship for ages, and my encounter with that guest had barely taken the edge off. Before I had time to consider what I'd do, the one on top turned and laughed.

'Hey Mark, he is in here,' he said.

Mark peered up over his shoulder at me.

'So there you are. Your brother said he thought we'd find you in the pool but when we saw you weren't there we thought we'd sneak in here to be alone but ... Well, what are you waiting for?' he said to me.

I didn't need to be asked twice, so I positioned myself behind the one on top, grabbed his hips, and pulled him up so I could manoeuvre my cock into his tight hole. Mark lunged for my balls and began to suck them into his mouth.

As much as I was enjoying it I didn't want to waste time in case someone came looking for us because I was needed for some reason, so I disengaged myself from Mark – reluctantly, I might add. I pushed the other guy forward so Mark could continue paying attention to his friend's cock and began to inch my cock in his hole.

'Oh fuck, that's awesome,' he said.

'I knew you'd love it,' Mark muttered, his mouth full.

I couldn't see Mark in this position but I felt his eyes on me, on the underside of my balls, and every now and again his tongue would lash out and lick at me. It was maddening. Part of me just wanted him to suck me off but the other part wanted to fuck his friend up the arse, and I guess his arse won because I was also hoping that later on that night we might be able to continue what we were starting here.

'Oh yeah, that's great,' he said again.

I held on to his hips, planning to go slow so as not to hurt him.

'Harder,' he demanded. 'We haven't got all day.'

'Fine by me,' I said, slamming it into him, the thrill of this unexpected encounter leaving me almost breathless.

His body was slick with perspiration and his back toned, the muscles rippling. His excitement built up quickly and before I knew it he was exploding into Mark's mouth. Mark licked and swallowed him down, enjoying the taste as it dribbled down his throat.

I slapped the guy on the arse, indicating I was finished with him, and as he moved Mark's mouth managed to find its way onto my shaft so I leant forward to taste his cock, wet from the other's mouth.

I slid in a finger as my tongue danced along his crack. He squirmed beneath me while the other one played around with my puckered hole, slathering it with saliva before inserting a finger. As I probed Mark he probed me. It was magical, but I knew I didn't have much time; my brother would get suspicious if I didn't hurry up and relieve him. Pulling away, I yanked Mark up and had him bend over the bench. He went wild with wanting, grabbed back at my cock, and dragged me to him. I pried open his puckered hole, eased in my knob then raked my fingers down his back, kneading his muscles as I went. He moaned and the other guy ran his hands over me, cupping my balls, which were threatening to explode.

'Oh fuck, man, where did you learn how to fuck like that?' Mark asked as the other guy began to jerk him off, all the while checking out my rigid cock as it slipped in and out.

Before long I was coming, shooting high in him as he too exploded, throwing his head back, thrusting his cock into the other guy's hand as he screamed in ecstasy.

We collapsed, me on Mark's back, while we regained our composure and breath.

The other guy lunged for me, to take me in his mouth, but I shook my head.

'Not now, I can't,' I said. 'But let's meet again later

and we can relax and enjoy ourselves better.'

Quickly pulling on my bathers, I made them promise to return again later that night and this time I'd let them into the pool area where we could then lock the door. We'd be able to frolic and do as we wished in the heated pool and this time the only working out I'd do beforehand would be on the two of them.

This four-day conference was certainly going to do me and my own business a lot of good.

# In the Dark
## by Jerry Wilson

Every well-established gay pub or club worthy of the name has its special little dark room. It's usually the room out the back with the unmarked, nondescript door, where a regular trickle of people enters for a while. And when they come out again it's usually with satisfied smiles on their faces. At the Reclining Queen, things are not that different. There's no sign on the door, and entry is by reputation only – novices are just tossed in, tossed off, and tossed out again, all in double-quick time. It's where Johnny Fox goes when he feels in the mood for some serious high-grade oral sex, because he knows only too well that once behind that door the other regular visitors will know him as someone who has made a reputation for being an expert at it.

There are those people who will often describe themselves as a chocoholic. They are the people who feel they're addicted to the substance – they have urges and cravings that need to be sated. But Johnny, when he is in his guise as "Dr Fox", calls himself a serious, full-time cock-o-holic. The words are different, but the craving is still the same.

He's been one of the star attractions for as long as many can remember, and although there's no official fan club, he does have his regular crowd of followers, because although the dark room is like any one of the dozens you've probably visited in your time, Johnny always makes this one seem special. In reality, the room is dimly lit by a single tiny lightbulb above the door. There's a worn and filthy carpet on the floor, the walls are plain emulsion, and there are several tables arranged randomly in and near the corners of the room – all of them bolted down, as are the few tatty easy chairs. By the end of an average evening it's guaranteed that the floor will be littered with cigarette ends and empty popper bottles, used condoms and discarded sachets of lube. Plus the obligatory dark, wet patches of bodily fluids …

Yet the punters are happy to come and go, all safe in the knowledge of their anonymity if they feel they need it, for what happens behind the door stays behind the door. For some it's the supposed danger and excitement of it all, the adrenaline pressure of illicit sexual gratification with a total stranger, while for others it offers a chance to indulge in acts, desires, and fantasies which even their regular boyfriends have probably refused to be a part of.

But as Johnny Fox passes through the door and makes himself comfortable in his usual chair – untouched by anyone else, out of respect for the good doctor's hard-won reputation – the overriding smell is that of sexual tension and the promise of uninhibited sexual release. And Johnny knows his word-of-mouth advertising succinctly says it all. "Doctor Fox *really* sucks your cocks". And the doctor is in.

On the side table beside Johnny's chair he carefully puts down a small plastic bottle of some cheap diet cola and alongside it he puts another of still highland spring water, along with a plastic half-pint glass from the bar. With a twist of his wrist he breaks the seal on the water, rinses the glass out before pouring a little more into the beaker and drinking it. It's really just enough to whet

Johnny's appetite and he barely has any time to start limbering up and stretching his jaw muscles when the night's first prick steps up in front of him.

In the dim light the guy looks like some kind of a James Dean clone – all leather jacket, blue jeans, white T-shirt, and black boots. He unzips himself and takes out an average, standard-sized cock, neatly circumcised, which he slowly strokes and rubs a couple of times before presenting it for Johnny's inspection. For a moment the darkroom seems to go silent and still – Johnny's never refused any cock up to now, but there's always the first time. Johnny breaks the tension with a smile, and takes the cock in one hand while with the other he reaches in and pulls James Dean's balls out from behind the faded blue denim. As they sit in the palm of Johnny's hot, dry hand he can see that they're already starting to contract and tighten up. Not much of a challenge, but it's a start, and the night is still young. Johnny gives the cock a few more firm and slow strokes, then it's down to business, and he's bending his head forward in order to pop the stiff and throbbing prick into his hot and eager mouth. Within moments, Johnny is rolling his tongue around the tangy shaft and over the slippery cockhead – letting James Dean reach out and tentatively put his hands behind Johnny's head, even though Johnny has never needed a helping hand in his life. Still, it lets Johnny know that this James Dean is an obvious amateur and for once Johnny doesn't really have time for novices and beginners.

Taking control of the situation, Johnny brings both his hands around James Dean's hips and firmly grips and cups his tight arse. Then in precise, measured movements, Johnny physically pulls the guy towards him, deliberately taking the length of cock into his mouth and slipping it easily down his throat – two, three, four times – all in quick succession, until the cock is jerking and spitting large gobbets of come into Johnny's mouth.

A few good swallows and the first of the night's punters has been sucked dry before Johnny releases his hold. It was interesting, but then most canapés are designed to tease the taste buds, and whet the appetite, nothing more.

Spitting out the deflating cock, Johnny dismisses the inexperienced guy and settles back into the comfort of his chair again, his eyes steadily becoming more accustomed to the dimness. Over in one of the opposite corners there is a tall, well-built black guy. He's standing, with his face pressed hard up against the wall, hands outstretched and placed high up on the painted plaster, legs spread out as if waiting for a police search. He's wearing an old-fashioned plaid cotton shirt which has the sleeves rolled up a little way above the elbows – just enough to show some of his biceps. The shirt is complemented by a pair of well-worn blue denim bib-fronted overalls, and muddy work boots. It's a slave fantasy thing. He calls himself Marcus Sugarcane from Barbados, for obvious reasons, but his real name is Richard and he's been studying Social Politics at Cambridge for the last two years. The overalls have a large button down flap at the back which, when unbuttoned by some interested slave master, completely exposes his hot and taut black arse. Around his feet there are already half-a-dozen used condoms of various colours and sizes. Marcus from Barbados will take any cock, but not if it's bareback.

Rumour has it that he has a foot of thick black mamba snake curled up snugly in his jock box. But none of his punters is ever allowed to touch it. The thought makes Johnny smile wistfully, because he's one of the few to know from experience that it's only nine inches, but tastily thick, and with great swinging balls to match.

But there is no time for Johnny to be reminiscing. Far from it, in fact, as the next guy in an informal queue steps in front of him – effectively blocking Johnny's clear view of Marcus – and proceeds to unzip himself. It's a nice piece of Indian or Asian meat, as fragrant and inviting as cardamom rice. Johnny purses his lips a little, savouring the moment like a boa constrictor. The cock has been very nicely circumcised, with the circular scar creating a beautiful presentation ring, but, when Johnny deftly eases in and lifts the golden-brown balls out, he discover that this guy is completely shaven – making his balls and the base of his cock all the more sensitive than if it were still *au naturel*. Johnny licks his lips several times before slipping just the head of this tasty cock into his mouth and tickles the piss-slit with the firm tip of his tongue. Then, with a long intake of breath, he settles himself into a steady, rhythmical routine of slowly moving his head up and down the shaft.

But then sensuous dark fingers reach out and gently take hold of both sides of Johnny's head, their pressure clearly indicating Johnny should stop his movements. Johnny waits a second or two to see what this punter is up to – all the while hoping it will be something unusual and different, which would make for a very pleasant surprise.

As if on cue, the Maharajah slowly starts to move his hips in a sensuous, circular motion, almost dance-like, so that his cock is drawn out of Johnny's mouth – though leaving the head still remaining pressed up against his lips – and then slides back in deeply, almost down into Johnny's throat. He relaxes into the experience, safe in the knowledge that he is being head-fucked by another artist, and from the corners of his half-closed eyes he can see the pair of them are gaining an appreciative audience.

Three or four of other punters are standing close by, eagerly watching how the action is going, and from their own movements Johnny knows they already have their own cocks out and are wanking themselves – or each other – off. With a practised hand, Johnny picks up the plastic half-pint beaker and taps it several times in quick succession on the tabletop before going back to working on the experienced cock in his ready mouth.

With his head still held by the Maharajah's firm hands, the only things left for Johnny to use are his energetic tongue and slippery lips. Expertly he curls and holds his tongue so that it rubs and strokes against the underside of this tasty cock. To heighten the sensations he also firms his lips into a tight ring around the shaft, matching his efforts in time with the rhythmical strokes, which are now getting faster and faster as the Maharajah's excitement keeps building. To help him get off, Johnny deliberately brushes his fingertips lightly on the underside of the gloriously shaven, light brown ball sack – making the Maharajah twitch and grunt loudly with pleasure. So much so that, without any encouragement, he starts to pull Johnny's head further onto his cock. From lightly tickling, Johnny switches to deliberately cupping and fondling the hot balls in the palm of his hand, delighted at feeling them draw up tightly – almost inside himself – while his hips start to frantically thrust into Johnny's face. A distant second or two later and his hips and groin are twisting and jerking in pleasure as his orgasm explodes within him, gushing out in forceful spurts, filling Johnny's mouth full of his hot, salty come.

As the grunting dies down, Johnny politely waits for him to recover; taking a little time to lick the final traces of sticky juice from the Maharajah's cock before letting him put it safely back into his well-cut designer trousers.

Once he's zipped himself back up he nods a silent "thank you" before he walks away, heading back through the door and into the pub again. Another satisfied customer well serviced.

Relaxing a little, it's time for the doctor to take a short break. Settling back again, Johnny takes a look at the plastic half-pint beaker now sitting back on the table, a warm smile on his face as he sees that it's nearly a third full with come. Good boys, they've never let the doctor down yet. In this church the congregation are more than willing to give generously.

Knowing that more than a few pairs of eyes are watching him, he reaches over and breaks open the small bottle of diet cola. With a slow, steady hand, he carefully start to pour – topping the plastic container up with the dark brown liquid, the bubbling head threatening to overflow. Letting it settle for a moment, he deliberately picks it up and then downs the whole come and cola concoction in one. It's the only way Johnny knows of putting the cock back into cocktails. And if anyone should ask him, he'll tell them that he calls it a Jizz Fizz – usually one part hot sperm to two parts cola.

With nobody immediately in front of him, he gets a chance to take a long look at how things are with Marcus over by the opposite wall, just in time to settle back and watch as a large black guy step up behind him. He wastes no time in whipping out his own impressive uncut cock – the glorious cockhead flashing pink and bright against the dark meat – before he lubes the tip up, puts on a condom, and slams into Marcus so hard that he staggers forward a little when his feet are almost lifted off the floor.

The change of fantasies for Marcus is easy. Slave and master, prison guard and first-timer, cop and gangsta. But even Johnny knows that Marcus has had more meat inside him than a butcher's dog. He's a craftsman, and his technique is so good that the other guy is coming in a matter of a few short minutes – snorting like an angry bull and pushing Marcus Sugarcane hard against the wall.

Black on black action is a turn-on for some, and no sooner is that show over than another large, leather-jacketed black guy – the angry bull's boyfriend? – is in front of Johnny, offering up his own piece of solid dark meat. Ebony black and musky, surrounded by tight pubic hair, this one is also gloriously uncut, with the pinkish, large head glistening and oozing precome.

He very rarely gets to handle this kind of quality and so naturally Johnny decides he's definitely going to take his own sweet time over it. He starts by a little teasing – gently tugging on the shaft to ease the half-stretched foreskin further back down the head, letting it almost slip behind the rim, but not quite, so that it slides back up again as soon as he takes the pressure off. Carefully he lifts the shaft up so he can get this guy's balls out, freeing them one at a time until they look like large black eggs sitting so nicely in the palm of his hand. They are so inviting that Johnny bends forward and kisses both of them once, before slowly running his tongue up the whole length of rigid shaft to tickle and flick the very tip of it in and out of his pinkish piss-slit.

Now as Johnny pulls the flexible foreskin back he runs his firm tongue around and over the head, rolling it under the rim, before purposefully sinking down on it like some cock-hungry giant anaconda devouring its prey. He can't unhinge his jaw, but Johnny automatically opens up the back of his throat and greedily tries to swallow as much of the shaft down as he can. As for the rest? He slowly starts moving his head a little up and down while he also begins to wank the well-endowed guy off with his hand –

this shaft is gratifyingly too big even for Johnny's experienced and skilful mouth.

Time to take it up a notch or two, and Johnny rolls the firm black balls around his palm once more before he starts to rhythmically tug gently downward on them, careful not to exert too much pressure at first – this is, after all, mutual pleasure, not some BDSM session. Getting more into the moment, the guy starts to breathe heavily, purposefully putting his hands on his hips and leaning back a little at the waist. It not only gives Johnny a lot more freedom for him to really work his magic, it also gives the appreciative little crowd of onlookers a much better view of the action. Out of the corner of Johnny's eye he sees his plastic tumbler already being passed around the group of masturbating aficionados. Ah yes, all donations kindly received – especially by a notorious spunk-hound such as Johnny Fox!

Yet there is little time to waste, and as Johnny works on those glorious balls he knows he can feel them starting to move and tighten up, and under his fingers he can feel the solid length of cock getting that pre-ejaculation iron-hard stiffness he has come to know so well. This fucker is just about to blow his wad!

Deliberately he starts to push back, and Johnny start to quicken his hand on the veined shaft, sliding the pinkish cockhead out from the back of his throat so as not to choke on the impending flood of juices. Up and down with his firm fingers, up and down with his hot mouth, flick, flick, flick with the tip of his tongue and suck, suck, suck with his tight lips until the guy all but jerks his cock out of Johnny's mouth with the first fire-hose blast of come. Thankfully Johnny manages to hold on to the twitching and jerking wild cock and he has barely enough time to swallow and gulp down the first gushing shot before the second and then the third are filling his mouth to bursting and beyond.

Finally, Johnny lets the pulsating cock slip out of his mouth, and there is low murmur of appreciation from the gathered onlookers. Someone nearby quickly offers him a Kleenex tissue and he spends several moments sopping up the jism from the corners of his mouth, while still enjoying the feeling of it dribbling down his chin. When Johnny's finished, a hand reaches out and takes the crumpled tissue away; probably it will become a souvenir of the night's action…

Looking down at the table, Johnny sees he has all the makings of another Jizz Fizz. Ah, good boys …

Yet time has ticked by while he's been enjoying himself. It's almost closing time and the evening is virtually complete – even the most dedicated punters are slowly moving off to the all-night clubs or other equally disreputable fuck palaces. The door to the darkroom is wedged open, the few other ceiling lights turned on, and the bar staff start to do a very cursory tidying up – just sweeping the detritus off into a corner so someone else can clean it up tomorrow.

As Marcus Sugarcane and Johnny Fox leave, the landlord calls them both over and pays each for their evening's work. Their notoriety and reputations are partially responsible for bringing in the punters, and that's what keeps the landlord in business, despite the fact he probably knows the pair of them would be more than willing to do it all for free.

Later still, when both Marcus and Johnny are wrapped around each other in their large double bed, they both slowly tease, stroke and wank each other to sleep, happy in the knowledge that tomorrow night it will start all over again.

## Short Orders
### by E.C. Cutler

I only took Riley on because I was desperate for a bus boy. The guy who'd had the job before him, Dan, had quit for a better-paid job earlier in the week, and I needed someone to clear tables, wash the dishes, and help out in the kitchen at busy times. The place might only have been small, with room for no more than half-a-dozen customers to sit at the counter, and a couple of booths at the far end, but that just meant it was important to keep on top of things. I pride myself on being a pretty decent short-order cook, and at weekends the line for a seat in the diner would stretch out of the door. Marie, my regular waitress, had worked for me for close on five years now, and she was a real treasure, but she couldn't do everything. So when Riley walked into the diner late one Friday afternoon to ask if I had any work available, my first thought was that he could prove to be a real life-saver.

My second thought was that he was the most gorgeous guy I'd seen in a long time, with a muscular frame beneath his tight T-shirt and low-slung jeans. He kept pushing his tousled blond hair out of his eyes with long, slender fingers, and his eyes were the soft green of summer moss. Forget waiting tables; the guy could make it as a romance cover model. My dick twitched to attention, even as I tried to convince myself I was making the decision to employ him with my head, rather than my lower portions.

'You won't regret this, Mr Anderson, I promise you,' Riley assured me.

'Call me Gray,' I told him, shaking hands on the deal. 'And I'll see you tomorrow.'

He was 20 minutes late that first Saturday, which should have been a warning sign for what was to come.

The breakfast rush was just starting. His tasks were simple: keeping the counter and the tables in the booths clear of dirty plates, and refilling coffee cups if Marie was working the cash register. He nodded at my instructions, tucking his hair beneath the white paper hat he was required to wear and fastening an apron around his waist, though I noticed he didn't attack the job of wiping down the tables with much enthusiasm.

'Who's the hottie?' Marie asked, picking up two plates of eggs over easy and home fries for the couple in the far booth.

'That's Riley Barnes. He rolled up last night just as I was closing up, looking for work.'

Marie patted her dark curls. 'Honey, if I was 20 years younger, the kid wouldn't stand a chance.'

You and me both, I thought, but I said nothing. That night in bed, though, I wrapped my fist round my cock and jerked off to images of Riley on his knees, wearing nothing but that cute paper hat as he deep-throated me.

It was a delicious fantasy, and one that would torment me for many nights to come, just as Riley tormented me during the day.

It didn't take me long to realise employing Riley had been a grade-A mistake. He regularly turned up late for work, and when he did arrive he put as little effort into the job

73

as was humanly possible. I would glance up from the stove to see him checking his reflection in the mirrored surface of the espresso machine, or outside on the sidewalk, taking a cigarette break when he should be clearing tables. Whenever I called him into the kitchen to wash up before the stack of dirty plates threatened to topple into the sink, he did so with a distinct lack of grace, as though I'd interrupted him in the middle of something much more important. He wasn't exactly rude to the customers, but he never greeted them with the smile or the cheery words that were Marie's stock in trade. The number of teenage girls who came in after class finished for the afternoon, lingering over a milk shake, had increased significantly since Riley started working for me, but though they all did their best to catch his eye, flirting and chattering, he didn't seem to pay attention to any of them. I just put it down to his general contempt for my customers.

'This is such a lame place to work,' he complained on more than one occasion. 'Hell, this is a lame town.'

'So why are you here, if you hate it so much?' I asked him.

'In case you haven't noticed, there aren't many jobs around at the moment if you don't have much in the way of qualifications.' Somehow, he still managed to make it sound like he was the one doing me a favour.

I was prepared to overlook his tardiness and all his many other faults, until the week the cash register came up light three days in succession. The amount was only down by a few dollars each time, and I couldn't prove anyone was taking money from the till, not yet, but I had my suspicions.

They were confirmed when we were clearing up on the Friday night, Marie chattering about her plans to go to the

74

movies at the drive-in over in Mendon with her husband. When she went to use the ladies' room, she left her purse on the counter. Coming back from stowing leftovers in the cold store, I was shocked to see Riley quietly reaching into Marie's purse and extracting her wallet. He'd removed a couple of $10 bills and was in the process of slipping the wallet back where it had come from when I stepped out from behind the counter.

'Stealing from a co-worker, Riley? That's low.'

Riley tried to laugh the accusation off, but his body language was defensive. 'What the fuck are you talking about, man?'

'I saw you, so don't bother trying to deny it. First you take money from the cash register, then you take it from Marie. Who was next, me?'

'Take what from Marie?' She'd emerged from the restroom without either of us noticing.

'I caught him going through your purse,' I informed her. 'Don't you think you should hand back what you took, Riley?'

Expecting him to keep denying what he'd done, I was surprised instead to see him slip the two bills from his back pocket and return them to Marie.

'I hope you're going to call the cops, Gray.' Marie tucked the money into her purse and reached for her coat.

'It doesn't have to go that far, does it, Riley? I'm sure we can sort out this out between us.' Though part of me wanted to see Riley hauled down to the station, maybe even spend a night in the cells for the way he'd behaved, I had the feeling that wouldn't solve the underlying issue. 'Maybe an apology to Marie would be in order?'

'Sorry, ma'am,' he mumbled, though I was sure the only thing he was sorry about was the fact he'd been caught in the act.

For a moment, I thought Marie wasn't going to accept the apology; that she'd continue to press for me to get the police involved, or at the very least fire Riley on the spot. Then a car horn hooted outside. 'Oh, that'll be Charlie.'

'You run along, Marie. Enjoy your evening. I can take care of things from here.'

She still looked doubtful, but I ushered her out into the street, watching as she climbed into the cab of her husband's pick-up. Once she'd gone, I locked the door of the diner and turned to Riley.

'Now, I bet you're wondering why I didn't do what Marie wanted, and call the cops. By rights I should. Did you really think you could steal from me and get away with it?'

'Oh, come on, man. What's a few dollars here and there?'

'To a company like McDonalds, maybe, very little. But I don't have anything like their profit margins, Riley. It doesn't take much to put a place this size out of business. Didn't you know that, or didn't you care?'

Riley snorted. 'I wouldn't even be here if there were any decent jobs out there. But unless you've got a college degree, no one even looks at you. So you end up stuck in a lame place like this, working all the hours God sends, scraping by on the minimum wage.'

He might have had a point, but I was tired of his self-justifying whining. I'd done any number of low-paying, soul-destroying menial jobs when I'd first left high school, and I wasn't prepared to stand here and let Riley damage everything I'd worked so hard to achieve.

'Spare me the sob story,' I snapped, 'and give me one good reason why I shouldn't just fire you right now …'

'Please, Gray. I'm sorry.' Riley sounded surprisingly contrite, for someone who was about to lose a job he didn't like very much. 'I know I shouldn't have taken money from you, or Marie. I promise I'll make it up to you somehow.'

He ran a hand through his floppy hair. His cocky self-assurance was melting away by the second and, despite my anger, my cock was swelling in my pants at the sudden measure of control I had over him.

'You know, Riley,' I said, voice calm and level, 'I think the real problem here is that you lack any kind of discipline in your life. You think you can turn up here when you feel like it, do as little work as you can get away with; treat people like they're something you scraped off your shoe. Well, you need to be taught otherwise. And the cops might not be able to hand out that kind of lesson – but I can.'

Riley glanced round, a panicked expression in his wide, green eyes. For the first time, he was starting to realise the two of us were alone here. I'd already pulled down the blinds, so no one passing would have a view of whatever might be about to happen.

'What – what are you going to do to me?' he asked.

'Something your dad should probably have done a long time ago. You need to have some sense beaten into you, kid.'

'Oh, come on, you're joking, right?' From the look on his face, I guessed he was debating whether he'd be better off handing himself over to the police. I'd almost have felt sorry for him, if I didn't know he deserved everything that was about to come to him.

I shook my head. 'You're clearly overdue a spanking, and it's time I put that right.'

As I spoke, I looked round for the perfect tool to dish out his punishment. I could use my hand, of course, but I wanted to really give him a spanking to remember, and that required something like a paddle, or a ping-pong bat, or –

My eyes must have lit up when I saw the wooden spatula lying on the counter by the grill, because Riley gave an involuntary shudder. I closed my fingers round the implement, smiling as I swished it through the air.

'OK, man, this has gone far enough,' Riley said, but his protest sounded half-hearted, almost as if, deep down, he craved the feel of that spatula on his butt.

I wanted him over my lap for his spanking – it seemed the most appropriate position, one that would reinforce his humiliation and sense of shame. There was an old, wooden-backed chair in the corner – Marie sometimes used it to sit on when she was on a break – and I dragged it out into the clear floor space in the middle of the kitchen.

'Right, Riley, drop your pants,' I ordered him, once I was seated. When he hesitated, I added, 'Unless you want me to do it for you?'

The threat seemed to galvanise him. He unbuckled his belt, before making short work of his fly buttons. As he stepped out of his jeans, I took a moment to admire the lean lines of his tanned thighs, and the nice-looking package concealed in his tight-fitting white briefs. Somehow, that innocent-looking underwear only added to his bad boy aura.

He stood, lips set in a sullen pout, hands clasped together over the bulge in his briefs. I patted my lap. 'Make yourself comfortable, Riley.'

He took a slow pace forward, then another, trying to string out the moment when he'd have to lay himself over my thighs for as long as possible.

'Come on, I haven't got all day.'

At last, I had him in place, those gorgeous buns of his,

covered in tight white cotton, within easy swatting distance. I ran the spatula over each of his cheeks in turn, crooning softly, 'Such a luscious, ass, Riley. So ripe and firm and round. Just made to be spanked …'

He didn't say a word, but I swore I felt his cock twitch where it was trapped between our two bodies. I was sure he was starting to think this wasn't going to be so bad, after all.

'I wish I didn't have to do this,' I continued, raising my arm, 'but you've really left me with no other choice.'

With that, I brought the spatula down hard on his ass, the sharp crack of wood meeting flesh echoing round the cramped kitchen. 'Shit!' Riley hissed, clearly caught out by the force of the stroke.

'Now, Riley, what kind of language is that? Consider another two swats added to your punishment for not being able to control your tongue.'

Until I said that, I hadn't even thought about giving him a set number of strokes, but now it seemed to make sense. An even 20, the same as the amount he'd tried to lift from Marie's wallet, with a couple on top for his unnecessary curse word. I didn't make him count them, just concentrated on making sure that they covered both of his cheeks evenly, not leaving an inch of skin untouched. He bore the punishment in as close to silence as he could manage, though the odd yelp slipped from his lips when the spatula landed on a spot I'd already slapped.

With six strokes still to go, I paused. He must have thought that was the end of the proceedings, because he tried to rise from my lap. Applying my hand firmly to the small of his back prevented him from going anywhere.

'Not so fast,' I told him. 'There's still another six to come. Let's just see what that ass of yours looks like, shall we?'

I grasped the waistband of his briefs, peeled them down slowly despite Riley's protests. The flesh of his ass was mottled red, and noticeably warm to the touch. My cock was hard and, when I reached a hand underneath myself to check, I discovered his was getting there. I noticed that he didn't pull away, or threaten any kind of retribution, when I stroked his dick. Whatever else he might have had a problem with, he liked the feel of me wanking him.

'OK, let's get back on with this ...'

If he was hoping I'd pull his briefs up again, he was sorely disappointed. I left them bunched around the tops of his thighs. The remainder of his punishment would be given on his bare ass.

Now, if anything, I laid the strokes on harder than before, so hard I was afraid the spatula might actually split in two. His ass slowly turned a deeper shade of red, like late season plums and just as sweet. Riley howled as I dished out the last two swats, promising me he'd learned his lesson; he'd never steal again and he'd do anything I wanted, just as long as I stopped spanking him.

When it was over, I dropped the spatula to the floor. My arm ached, and my cock was a solid bar in my pants. Riley climbed down off my lap, but instead of pulling his tighty-whities back up, he dropped to his knees between my wide-spread legs. Almost before I knew what was happening, he'd unzipped my fly, reaching inside to bring my cock out. His lips, formed in a perfect O, closed around my helmet, and I nearly shot everything I had. Only a great effort of will prevented me coming in that moment.

Riley began to suck, supple lips moving up and down every inch of my shaft. He wasn't doing this because he felt he had to; he wanted to suck me off. From the way his tongue lapped at the sensitive spot just beneath my crown, he'd done this before. Realisation dawned on me, and I wondered how I could have been so blind. Riley hadn't ignored the girls who flirted with him because he was being rude; he simply wasn't interested in women.

He took me deeper, till it seemed I was lodged all the way down his throat and my bush was practically tickling the end of his nose. There's nothing you can do when you're receiving a blowjob as expert as the one Riley was giving me except sit back and enjoy it, and that's what I did. Through half-closed eyes, I watched his blond head bobbing up and down on my dick, already feeling the spunk rising from my balls.

Riley took hold of his own cock, fisting it as he brought me ever closer to the brink. Try as I might to hold back, to make the pleasure last just a few delicious moments longer, I was fighting against the tide. Every nerve ending in my body tight, I surrendered to the pull of Riley's skilled, relentlessly sucking mouth, and glazed his tonsils with my spunk.

Barely had he swallowed my load before I heard him cry out, and his own come was pumping out over his clenched fingers, thick and pearly.

We hardly said a word to each other as we cleaned ourselves off and dressed once more, and I fully expected this to be the last I ever saw of Riley. But when I unlocked the front door to let him leave, he paused on the threshold.

'Thanks for not firing my ass, Gray,' he said. 'I'll see you tomorrow, bright and early. And I'll work harder from now on. I know I haven't been the greatest employee you've ever had, but now I know what happens if I screw up …'

He didn't have to say anything. Despite all Riley's promises, I knew it probably wouldn't be too long before he did something to earn my displeasure again. And I knew we'd both enjoy the punishment he'd receive when he did.

## Lucky Buck
### by G.R. Richards

It wasn't just the squeak of mattress springs that drove Buck crazy. It wasn't the pounding of a heavy headboard against the shared wall either. It was the voices. The *men's* voices.

'You want it, twink?' the one guy asked. 'You want my fat cock in your ass?'

'Fuck yeah!' the other guy answered. 'Give it to me, Rod! I want you to fuck my ass all night long.'

'I'll fuck your ass until I say it's time to stop,' the first guy roared. 'I'll slap my fat cock across your skinny little face if that's what I want.'

And then, 'Do it! I dare you to whack me in the face with that big monster cock.'

And, 'Maybe I will, twink. Maybe I'll smack my dick all over your scrawny little body.'

The wall muffled their cries of ecstasy a little, but nowhere near enough. Those guys sounded so pathetic, and not because they were gay – Buck was hot for men too, so who was he to judge? – but because of their stupid dialogue. They kept saying the same damn things over and over again. It was like they were making a porno over there in the next apartment.

*Holy shit!* Buck sat straight up in bed and threw off the covers. *They're making a porno in the next apartment!*

Why had it taken him so long to put two and two

together? There was no other explanation, unless those guys were acting out a porn movie or something. No, no – Buck wanted to believe they were making a porno over there.

They were, weren't they?

Only one way to find out.

Slipping on a pair of flannel sleep pants, Buck stormed from his apartment without even bothering to lock the door. It wasn't until he'd knocked at the neighbouring apartment that he realised *shit! What am I gonna say when they answer?*

The door opened and a head poked out. This guy had a fuzzy beard and dark, unruly hair – not at all what Buck was expecting.

'Yeah?' the guy asked, eyeing Buck's naked chest. 'What do you want?'

For a second, Buck thought maybe he'd misheard, somehow. Maybe the gay porno noises were coming from a different apartment. In the hallway, he couldn't hear a thing.

And then he realised he'd been asked a question. What did he want? He was just about to say, 'Nothing,' apologise, and slink home when he happened to glance over the dude's mushroom cloud of hair, through the crack in the door, and into the neighbouring apartment.

A camera! A big, fuzzy microphone! This was the place, had to be the place. They really were making a porno in there.

The dude with the beard started to close the door, but Buck caught it by the handle. 'Wait,' he said.

'What?' the dude asked. He looked scared shitless. 'What do you want?'

Buck didn't really know what he wanted, so he just asked, 'Are you making a porno in there?'

Beardo inhaled sharply, then backed up a touch, letting the door open a little wider. 'Who wants to know?'

'I live next door,' Buck said. 'You're keeping me up.'

'So? What are you gonna do about it?' the guy asked, swallowing hard. 'Call the cops?'

Buck folded his arms across his bare chest and stared the guy down. Dude seemed to get smaller as the moments drove by, and finally he swung the door wide open. 'You can come in if you want.'

Buck couldn't conceal his smile. 'Thanks, man. I think I will.'

When the door closed, a bald guy in khakis and a polo shirt came out of the woodwork to shake Buck's hand. 'I'm Alto, the film's director. Please accept my apologies for keeping you … *up*?' The attractive older man winked, seeming to know exactly what Buck wanted. 'It's actually quite a boon that you've stopped by. You see, my models have tried our current scene time and again, and there's something missing. I wonder if …'

When Alto didn't finish his sentence, Buck said, 'Wonder what?'

With a snakelike smirk, Alto said, 'Oh, it's a silly idea. I'm sure you'll say no.'

'Well, still ask,' Buck probed, feeling itchy and desperate. His cock was already pummelling the inside of his sleep pants, getting ready for business. 'Maybe I'll say yes.'

Alto nodded deeply. 'Since you insist, I'm wondering if our scene would fare better with a third participant. Perhaps the character could be a furious neighbour who interrupts the action, and then – joins in?'

Buck's throat ran dry. This was exactly the offer he'd been hoping for, but now that it was set in his lap he felt so nervous he could have heaved. Was this stranger really offering him a role in a porno? Just like that? Seriously?

'But you haven't even seen my junk,' Buck said. 'Don't you want to, you know, get a glimpse?'

The bald man's eyebrows rose and a wicked smile appeared on his lips. 'Well, sure! Why don't you step into the bedroom and I'll introduce you to the boys? We'll all get a look at you together.'

When they entered the bedroom, the bearded man followed along, watching as Buck set his gaze on the pair of guys relaxing on the bed. Oh boy, Buck thought as his dick whacked his pyjama pants. This is gonna be some night!

He could tell easily enough which guy was "Rod" and which "the twink". Pulling out his earbuds and tossing his iPod in a drawer, the slim guy rose and introduced himself as Turner. Rod just nodded, but Buck could feel the guy's eyes blazing against his flesh as he pushed his pants down to the ground.

He stood before the four strangers completely naked.

And proud.

'So?' Buck asked. 'Did I get the part?'

'Goodness, yes!' Alto brushed his hands together as he explained how the scene should play out. Seemed straightforward enough to Buck, but he wouldn't know for sure until the camera was rolling. Turned out this was a pretty low-budget flick, so Alto did double duty as director and cameraman while the guy with the beard, whose name turned out to be Rutger, acted as soundman and gofer for the shoot.

When Alto called 'Action,' that was Buck's cue to knock at the door and re-imagine his stilted conversation with Rutger. This time it was Rod who opened the door, completely naked and hard as a steel girder.

In his character's gruff tone, Rod asked, 'Yeah? What

do you want?'

'I live next door,' Buck shot back, trying not to look at the camera. It wasn't too difficult when he had Rod's stern face and erect cock to ogle. 'I don't know what you're doing in there, but you're keeping me up.'

'I'll be the judge of that.' Pulling Buck inside by the waist of his pyjamas, Rod closed the apartment door. 'Let's get a look underneath these ugly-ass things.'

Buck didn't struggle when Rod pantsed him – it was all part of Alto's makeshift storyline.

'Well?' Buck asked, trying to sound cocky as he wrapped his fist around his hard-on. 'What do you think?'

Rod raised an eyebrow and set his hands on his hips, just like Mr Clean. 'I think we've done a damn fine job of keeping you *up*.' Then he called to Turner, 'Twink, get your scrawny ass in the living room. I've got a *job* for you.'

Wearing a dark terry robe, Turner walked into the living room and circled Buck. 'Well, what have we here?'

Buck gulped. Did he have a line to say? He hadn't acted since his fourth grade Christmas pageant, and he'd forgotten how tough it was to sound convincing saying someone else's words, much less remembering them.

'This guy's our neighbour,' Rod said, covering so they didn't have to restart the take. 'He says we've been keeping him *up* all night.'

'Well, something certainly has.' Turner grabbed Buck's biceps with both hands and squeezed. 'Don't worry, neighbour. You've *come* to the right place.'

'That's right,' Rod added as he pressed Buck down on the couch. 'My twink's gonna take good care of you.'

Buck swallowed hard, arranging the throw cushions behind his back so he could sit comfortably at the edge of the couch. 'OK, that sounds pretty good.'

'And while my twink's taking care of you,' Rod added, 'you can take care of me.'

By the time Turner dropped his robe, Buck had all but forgotten about the camera and microphone, the sound guy and director. He spread his legs so Turner could crawl between them, licking a path from his knee all the way up his thigh. Like a dog, the hot twink nuzzled his balls, and Buck could have sworn he heard sniffing.

With a laugh, Buck playfully smacked Turner's head. 'Are you smelling my crotch, kid?'

'So what if I am?' Turner shot back in a teasing tone. 'You got a problem with that?'

Rod flicked Turner's ear. 'Where are your manners, twink? Be polite to our neighbour.'

'Yes, sir,' Turner agreed. That perfect pink mouth was so close Buck could feel the guy's breath on his dick – and his dick reacted by whacking Turner in the face.

Rod laughed, and snapped Buck on the shoulder. 'Looks like someone's eager for a blowjob.'

Buck chuckled nervously. He didn't want to think about his erection, because if he thought too much maybe it would go away. And all this was being recorded! Wouldn't that be humiliating?

'Hey, neighbour,' Rod said, his voice like gravel. 'I asked you a question.'

'Huh?' Buck's heart raced in his chest. *What question?* He hadn't heard a question. 'You did?'

'Yeah, I did.' Rod took a step forward, his face like stone. 'I asked if you wanted a blowjob.'

Buck was pretty sure Rod had said that as a statement, not a question, but he wasn't going to argue. They were into improv now, and he didn't want to upset Alto by stopping the scene.

'Oh, I'm sorry,' Buck stammered. 'Yeah, yeah, I do

want my cock sucked. Sure I do.'

Running a rough hand through Turner's mop top, Rod said, 'You heard the man, twink. He wants you to suck his dick. So suck his dick, already!'

'Yes, sir.' Turner nodded between Buck's legs, catching his firm shaft between those wicked white teeth.

He didn't bite hard, but Buck felt the impression of every cruel fang enough to jerk away. 'Dude! Watch it, huh?'

'What did he do?' Rod asked.

This wasn't in the script – not that there really *was* a script. Buck just had to go with it, saying, 'Your twink bit me!'

'Oh, he did, did he?' Rod closed in on Turner, standing directly behind him. 'What the fuck do you think you're pulling, twink? You take a bite out of our neighbour?'

'It wasn't hard,' Turner whined, impersonating an irritable teenager. 'He's just a pussy.'

Rod's eyes turned dark as he said, 'Don't you dare call our neighbour a pussy! He's a guest in our home.'

Buck didn't know what to do or say, so he sat perfectly still, watching as Rod pulled Turner to his feet. It came out of nowhere when Rod cast a firm hand down on the boy's rear, but the sound of that slap echoed through the living room.

'I told you to suck our neighbour's dick, twink.' Rod flattened his palm and brought it down once more against Turner's ass. 'Are you gonna do what I say, or what?'

For a moment, there was only silence. Buck didn't even breathe. He had no idea what would happen next, though he should have known: Rod smacked Turner's ass in swift repetition, one spank after another, warming the boy's cheeks. Buck wished he had the camera's angle – he'd have loved to see that scrawny white ass turn red.

When Turner started whimpering against Buck's thigh, Rod said, 'Now suck our neighbour's cock.'

Without hesitation, Turner said, 'Yes, sir!'

The twink shifted, circling his tongue around Buck's cockhead. That sensation was so intense and so immediate, Buck had to censor it or he'd surely blow his load all over Turner's face. God, just the sight of that young guy wrapping his mouth around Buck's throbbing red tip was more than he could handle. He had to close his eyes or it would all be over, and Alto probably wouldn't be happy about that.

Once Buck had closed his eyes, the world became pure sensation. He was just one big dick getting sucked by the hottest mouth he'd ever had wrapped around him. And not just hot, but soft as silk. When his dickhead struck the back of Turner's throat and the boy built suction all around his shaft, he started moving. He couldn't help it. He thrust in Turner's mouth, seeking even more heat, even more rough, brutal suction.

Buck reached out to grab Turner's hair, but his hand met something else altogether. He opened his eyes to find Rod towering above him and standing arched across Turner's bowed body, within the confines of Buck's wide-open thighs.

'You like my twink's mouth?' Rod asked.

'Yeah,' Buck said, nervous as hell about what came next. 'Yeah, for sure.'

Rod moved in closer, cradling his massive, veiny dick in one hand. His whole body was turned slightly so the camera would get a good look at his muscled chest and ripped abs. He stroked the underside of his dick, and all Buck wanted to do was pounce.

'You ever sucked another man's dick, neighbour?'

Buck almost screwed up his line, but caught himself at

the last moment and said, 'Me? No, never.'

'Well, there's a first time for everything,' Rod said, wrapping his fist around the base of his cock. 'Stick out your tongue.'

Turner was still sucking like crazy under Rod's looming form. Buck could hardly concentrate for the sheer lustful pleasure, but he did as instructed and stuck out his tongue.

'Very good,' Rod said. 'You're a quick learner, unlike this twink down here.'

The twink down there responded by grabbing Buck's balls and squeezing them so hard he yelped.

'Hey, no misbehaving!' Rod leant back to give Turner a firm slap on the ass, which only made the guy suck and squeeze more viciously. Then, shifting his attention back to Buck, he said, 'Get ready, neighbour, 'cause here I come…'

Without wasting another moment, Rod traced the slit of his deep pink cockhead up and down Buck's tongue, spilling precome all over his taste buds, making him squirm against Turner's face. God, he wanted to suck that monster. He wanted Rod to ram it down his throat. It was only a matter of time, he figured. After all, they were making a porno over here.

'You want to suck it, neighbour?'

Buck nodded, but all he could say with his tongue extended was, 'Uh-huh!'

Turner went at him even harder in that moment, pumping his cock and sucking so relentlessly Buck arched against the throw pillows. Oh God, he was going to come before the scene was over! Turner must have known he was torturing Buck, but the little runt didn't stop. All Buck could do was silently chant, 'Don't come, don't come, not yet!'

'Suck it,' Rod insisted as he shoved his dick roughly down Buck's throat.

Gagging, Buck struggled to steady himself, but all he could find to grip was Turner's hair. Turner shrieked at the perceived act of violence while Rod swirled his dickhead around at the back of Buck's throat. It was too much happening all at once, and he lost himself inside the action. He had no choice but to make himself into a human sex doll – a mouth for sucking, a dick to be sucked. That's all he would be to whoever watched this porno, anyway. They'd never know he was a real guy with a real job, with pet fish and siblings and bills to pay, just like everybody else. That thought could have been depressing, but instead it was a release. Just for now, he wasn't anything but a dude sucking a huge cock and getting his cock sucked in turn.

He went at Rod with renewed vigour, wanting his audience to see how much he loved sucking dick. Rod held his head steady and just fucked the hell out of Buck's face, pounding the back of his throat until the tender flesh back there was clenched and raw. Buck tried to say something, say yes, but every sound came out as an impassioned screech.

Meanwhile, Turner grabbed his balls and not only squeezed them, but twisted. Buck yelped as the pain merged with some fucked-up form of pleasure, like fiery knots in his colon. He tried to jerk away, but Rod had him by the hair and, beyond that, he had Turner by the hair! What could he do? He doled it out just like Rod was doing. He thrust deep inside Turner's mouth, filling the twink's throat with dick, swirling it around in there before going back at it, pounding his cock into the poor kid's throat.

From behind the camera, which Buck had pretty much

forgotten about, Alto raised his hand and gave the signal. It was time to come. Buck had been holding back so hard that he wondered how the hell he was going to switch gears. The answer came from Rod, who wove his fingers together behind Buck's head and started grunting like an animal while he pounded Buck's tender throat. Turner caught on soon enough, moaning around Buck's cock like he'd never eaten anything so delicious.

But it wasn't just the noises that put him over the edge – it was the sight of these two naked men working away, and the knowledge that Alto and the sound guy were watching. Once this movie was finished, there would be thousands, maybe millions of guys jerking off while they watched hot, hard Rod come all over Buck's face.

Blast after blast of cream coated Buck's cheeks, forehead, nose. He clenched his eyes closed, but all he could see was Rod's cockhead erupting with jizz, over and over again. He relived that sordid moment as Turner twisted his balls, and that was it. Everything had built to this moment, and he let his come soar down the skinny twink's throat.

'Mmmm!' Turner said, humming around Buck's cock as spurt after spurt of jizz emptied from his spent dick.

And then Alto was saying, 'Cut! Great job, boys – or *jobs*, should I say?'

Turner laughed, backing through Rod's legs while the director handed Buck a warm towel to wash the come from his face.

'Beginner's luck,' Rod said, giving Buck a smack on the shoulder.

The guy was hard to read, but Buck decided to take it as a friendly tease and responded, 'Thanks. Boy, am I exhausted! I'll sleep well tonight.'

'Sleep?' Alto asked, and everyone laughed. 'We need to get our close-up shots. We've got at least a couple more takes ahead of us. You're not done yet, young man.'

For a second, Buck thought they must be teasing him. When he realised they weren't, and he would likely spend all night sucking and getting sucked … Well, what could he do but smile?

## Dreams Come True
## by Amber March

'Someone told me you were a dirty little slut who needed a hard cock in his arse at least once a day,' Patrick growled. 'Is that true?'

The man he had pinned face first against the wall by his own front door whimpered and trembled and shook his head. 'No, no it's not true.'

'It's not? So you're calling my friend a liar?'

'No, I'm not, I'm just s-saying…,' the man stammered.

'What are you just saying? You don't need a cock in your arse or my friend's a liar?'

'I don't n-need a c-cock in my arse.'

'You don't?' Patrick squeezed one rounded, peachy buttock through denim. He ground his erection slowly against the man's arse cleft.

'N-no, oh God … No.'

Patrick smirked viciously. He was a man for hire, if you will. He wouldn't refer to himself as a prostitute but rather a man who did things for the needy. He liked his job. He liked to dominate men who wanted it. Emphasis on the want. This guy was a little different and Patrick had been uneasy taking the job.

He had been told by a mutual friend, Harry, that Oliver, a thin, nerdy PhD student had uncharacteristically spilled his guts during a heavy drinking session. He had confided that he dreamed of a man taking him by force, against his will, and that protesting his violation would all be part of the fun. He longed to be dominated, restrained, and mastered.

Patrick wasn't sure. He'd needed a lot of persuading. There he was, six feet three of him and built like a brick shithouse. Suddenly grabbing hold of this student as he was leaving his apartment, shoving him against the wall and telling him he'd heard a story about him being a dirty little cock-slut had uneasy connotations for him. What if the guy cried rape?

Patrick didn't know how to make sure Oliver wanted it but Harry had assured him over and over again that Oliver would want everything he was given, but would protest anyway for the thrill of it.

Still Patrick wasn't convinced, but he couldn't deny that holding the bloke against the wall with his victim shaking against him made his cock hard. Just as long as it was with excitement and not fear that Oliver shook.

'OK then,' he said, and he reached to Oliver's shoulders and pulled the jacket down his arms, casting it away. Then he reached around to unbutton his shirt, taking his time. 'Well, my friend told me quite a tale about you.'

Oliver turned his head over his shoulder, pale cheeks flushed. 'He did?'

He was really quite a pretty specimen, dark-haired with large, doe-brown eyes blinking behind his glasses and the longest, thickest lashes Patrick had ever seen. His profile was delicate, his mouth small but with pouting, plump lips.

'Yes, he did.' Patrick discarded the shirt too and ran his hands down the slender arch of Oliver's spine, feeling goosepimples break out on the creamy skin. 'He told me all the things you like a man to do to you.'

Oliver licked his pink lips nervously. 'He was bullshitting you, I didn't ...'

'So you didn't tell him you like to be fingered long and deep with plenty of lube, did you?'

'N-no.'

'Uh-huh.' Patrick reached around the student's waist. He unfastened Oliver's belt slowly. 'You didn't tell him you liked a tongue in your arse making you so wet that it runs down your legs?'

Oliver gave a soft whine. Patrick plucked open one, two, three buttons and pulled his jeans apart. 'No.'

'OK, and finally, just to check, you absolutely didn't tell him that your hungry hole is always desperate for a big, hard cock?'

'No.' It was a soft cry. Oliver was panting hard. He gave a gasp as Patrick plunged a hand into his pants and cupped his cock through thin briefs.

'You're hard. Why?'

'I don't know.' Oliver tried to pull away. Patrick slammed him back against the wall.

'Is it because you like the feel of my hand around you and my cock against your arse?'

'No.'

Patrick's fingertips wandered down the shaft that grew steadily solid under his ministrations. He rubbed a thumb over the cock head and felt a wet spot bloom on the material of Oliver's briefs.

'Wet and leaking,' he noted with satisfaction.

Oliver squirmed in his grasp. He whimpered as Patrick jammed his hand down his briefs and started wanking him firmly. Oliver bucked into his touch, clawing at the wall, groaning, his cock heavy and straining in Patrick's grip.

'You lose control easily for a man who isn't a cock slut.'

'I – I ...' Oliver stammered, biting at his own hand to stifle his sounds.

'You – what?' Patrick kissed Oliver's shoulder with a smile. With his other hand, he reached into Oliver's briefs to cup his balls. They were small, the sac tight, shaven. Just the way Patrick liked it. His cock swelled harder. He had a feeling this was going to be a pleasure. He licked around Oliver's delicate ear and tugged at the lobe with his teeth. 'Here's what's going to happen. I'm going to undress you. I'm going to handcuff you. I'm going to explore your delightful little body with my hands and my mouth and then I'm going to fuck you until you scream. No matter how much you beg me, I'm not going to stop. Do you understand?'

Something like a sob tore from Oliver's throat. 'No,' he whispered. 'No.'

'Hmm, you're sticking to the script. He said you would. He said I had to fuck you until you came your brains out, no matter how much you begged for mercy.'

Oliver leant his forehead on the wall. He said nothing.

Patrick paused, hands still cradling the family jewels. He was still so long, Oliver glanced over his shoulder.

Patrick craned forward, pressed a light kiss to the corner of Oliver's mouth. Oliver caught his breath. He turned his head further until their lips collided.

It was a soft, surprisingly satisfying kiss. No tongues, no demands, just gentle caressing. Patrick drew back, somewhat unsettled. 'You're a romantic.' He made it sound like a dirty word.

Oliver closed his eyes. 'Yes.'

'A soft little twink.'

Oliver said nothing. Patrick waited a moment more and then he wrenched down Oliver's jeans and briefs. 'You're not going to get romance here, so forget it.'

Oliver leant both arms on the wall above his head. He hissed, his firm, pale buttocks quivering as Patrick slapped one and then the other, leaving red handprints. He grasped Oliver by each wrist, pulled his arms down and behind his back, cuffed them together.

'Please, sir …?'

Patrick stared. *Sir*? He grinned, his prick growing ever harder. 'Well?'

'My friend didn't say I liked to be spanked too, did he?'

'No, he didn't. I added that one myself because you seem like the sort of dirty boy who would appreciate it.' And Patrick slapped his arse again.

Oliver jerked and hissed. His arse cheeks flamed. He lifted each foot willingly when Patrick crouched down and dragged off shoes, socks, jeans, briefs. He stood looking at Oliver's slender, naked body with his cock throbbing. Nice. Very fucking nice. This one was going to be so good. If he could be sure. He hesitated again before he cupped Oliver's throat, turning his head so he could reach his mouth once more.

Oliver kissed him with a soft sigh. Patrick removed the student's glasses, laid them down on the little table by the front door next to which they currently stood. While they kissed, Patrick unfastened his pants and shoved them down. He was naked beneath, seeing as this titillated some of his clients. Slowly and purposefully, he rubbed his cock up and down the split of Oliver's buttocks.

Oliver moaned into his mouth. He kissed Patrick feverishly, head craned right around over his shoulder so he could give Patrick's mouth his full attention.

Patrick pulled back. He felt light-headed and his hand shook when he dug in his pocket for condom and lube. Who was in control here? It seemed the little twink had him by the balls.

Angrily, he kicked Oliver's ankles apart. 'Wider. Let me see.'

Oliver groaned. The lube had a nozzle on the end. Patrick spread Oliver's plump buttocks with one hand. He pushed the nozzle tip into the tiny little hole and squirted.

Oliver squealed. Patrick used half the tube and withdrew. 'Your greedy little hole's all wet and dribbling, just begging to be fucked,' he said, watching lube sliding down Oliver's inner thighs.

Oliver shifted against the wall, pulling at his cuffs. He whimpered as Patrick pushed a finger inside him.

'Shit, you're tight. You're not going to be so tight when I've finished with you.'

Oliver panted and moaned, his ribcage heaving. 'Please, please … Stop.'

Patrick laughed. 'Stop? You're joking, aren't you? My cock's so hard I'm going to explode the moment I'm inside you. Are you really going to deny me the tightest, most delicious little arse I've ever seen?'

Oliver turned his head, a shocked expression on his blushing face which led Patrick to thinking. This man wasn't often the recipient of compliments. He was shy, retiring, and he never got laid. Those were Patrick's conclusions and what a damn shame it was that someone as delightful as Oliver was so neglected.

He fucked Oliver slowly with his finger, a mouth against his ear. 'Have you been fucked before?'

'Yes.'

'Did you or did you not tell your friend that you wanted a man to use your body until you couldn't take any more, no matter how much you begged him to stop?'

Oliver whimpered and closed his eyes. 'It was … I was drunk.'

'You were drunk and horny and wanted your sweet little hole filling.'

Oliver's thick lashes fluttered. He licked his lips nervously. 'I … Yes.'

'And I've been sent to do that.' Patrick crooked his finger forward, pressed lightly on Oliver's prostate.

Oliver jerked as though electrified. 'Oh my God!'

Patrick smiled and kissed his neck. He massaged and rubbed and felt Oliver's legs buckle and shake as though he'd fall down and then he grabbed his tumescent cock and placed it in the palm of one of Oliver's cuffed hands.

'Feel that. That's for you.'

Oliver's fingers squeezed. He moaned loudly. 'Oh God, I can't …'

'You can't?'

'Let me go, please!'

Patrick tutted. 'Silly boy. When are you going to admit you need me inside you?'

Oliver ground his teeth. 'I'm not, I'm not, let me go, you prick!'

Patrick growled. This was more like it. He had got as silly and soft as Oliver for a minute. Protest was much more of a thrill. He withdrew his finger and slapped Oliver's arse hard, earning a shrill yell.

He rolled on his rubber quickly and slicked the remainder of the lube over it. Then he gripped Oliver's hips and pulled them back, so Oliver's face was against the wall and his arse was sticking out in invitation.

Spreading the rosy buttocks with both hands, he rested his cock between them, rubbing it tantalisingly over the wet entrance. He pressed his face against Oliver's neck, kissed the light bristles of shaved hair and inhaled his scent. Yes, this was a nice one. He wouldn't forget Oliver in a hurry.

Oliver shouted as Patrick slid slickly inside, not stopping until he was sheathed all the way.

'Fuck,' he muttered, face against Oliver's neck, kissing. 'Oh God, you're good, boy.'

Oliver moaned deliriously. His cuffed hands felt for and rubbed Patrick's taut abdomen. 'I'm not a boy, you bastard.'

Patrick slapped his arse. 'If I say you're a boy, you're a boy. Behave yourself or I'll punish you.'

Oliver squirmed. 'Uncuff me, it hurts.'

'That's the idea. Now shut up.' Patrick started to ride him. Slow, steady strokes, plundering his slick insides, and Oliver moaned like a whore, trembling, gasping, and generally making enough noise to wake the dead. He should be a porn star, Patrick thought. A nice body, a tight arse and just the right sort of noise to get the viewers off. Certainly Oliver's sounds were getting him off just fine. He reached around and closed his hand around Oliver's good-sized cock.

'You're still hard considering you don't want it.'

Oliver said nothing. He just continued to moan as Patrick fucked him. Their skin stuck together with sweat. Oliver started to really get into it, pushing his hips back, impaling himself deeply on Patrick's cock.

'You slut, you little cock slut,' Patrick said, because Harry had told him that Oliver wanted to be verbally abused during this little fantasy of his. Called lots of filthy names because it would get him off. 'You love it, don't you, my big, hard cock in your greedy come-sucking hole?'

Oliver whimpered. 'Yes,' he said. 'Yes.'

Patrick squeezed his cock. 'Whore. *My* whore.'

Oliver bucked into his hand then back onto his cock. 'Yes. Use me. Make me yours.'

Patrick bit him savagely on the neck. He thrust hard into him. 'Let me feel that tight little hole clenching me.'

Oliver obliged by squeezing his impressive muscles. Patrick groaned. 'You're mine. My slut. I'm going to use your hole until you beg me to stop.'

Oliver was getting right in on the act now, much more enthusiastic than Patrick had ever anticipated. 'I need a cock inside my dirty little arse all the time,' he said. 'Give it to me. Fuck my brains out. Punish me.'

Patrick's hand tightened on his hip, his other around Oliver's cock. He slammed into Oliver as he wanked him furiously.

Oliver panted, filthy words continuing to spill from his tongue. 'I need you to come in my arse. I want to feel your spunk running from my hole and down my legs.'

Patrick caught his breath in shock. He'd done plenty of dirty things in his life but no one had ever asked him for this. He didn't even pause to consider.

He pulled out, stripped off his condom, and plunged back inside.

Oliver yelled. 'Fill me, oh God, fill my arse!'

Patrick roared. He buried himself as deep as he could go, spurting for England, wad after wad creaming Oliver's willing arse before he slumped forward, letting his lover's body hold him up a moment.

Oliver's back heaved against his chest. He moaned softly.

Patrick tongued the bruise he'd left on his neck. 'You filthy little bastard,' he said affectionately.

'That's right,' said Oliver. 'Now why don't you look at the mess you've made?'

Patrick caught his breath in renewed excitement. He eased himself free, dropped to his knees and spread Oliver apart.

Semen dripped from his still-twitching hole and streaked his thighs.

'I should make you go out like this,' Patrick said. 'Wearing no underpants so my come trickles down your legs and people see.'

Oliver gave a soft whine. He spread his legs further in deliberate invitation.

'Don't think I don't know what else you told Harry,' Patrick said. 'That you fantasised about being strapped down and used by a group of men, over and over until your hole's running with come and they take turns to lap it from you.'

Oliver hid his face. He said nothing, but his legs shook and his arsehole pulsed.

Patrick licked a line of white from Oliver's inner thigh. Oliver cried out. He pressed his arse back eagerly into Patrick's face.

Patrick slapped one cheek and then the other. Oliver jolted and shouted. Patrick did it again. He spanked and spanked until both cheeks were glowing and he listened to Oliver's steadily peaking cries and moans.

'You like to be spanked, don't you?'

'No.'

'Yes you do, just like you like something in your arse.'

'Please …,' Oliver burst out suddenly.

'What?'

'I need to come.'

'Do you? Perhaps I've exhausted myself fucking your tight arse.'

'Oh God, please!'

Patrick smiled to himself. 'What's in it for me?'

'I don't know. You can fuck my arse for the rest of the day. Or I'll suck your cock and let you come on my face. You can tie me up and spank me until I scream. Only please, just once, let me come. Please, sir.'

Patrick squeezed one flaming cheek. 'I *am* going to fuck your arse for the rest of the day. You can count on that. In fact, I'm going to come back every day for a week and fuck you until you can't stand up.'

Oliver whined and whimpered. 'Yes,' he said.

'Yes,' Patrick agreed and he meant it, no matter how many prior engagements he had. 'Now scream for me.' He held Oliver's buttocks apart and licked his wet hole ferociously.

Oliver did as he was told. His legs shook so hard Patrick used his shoulders to keep him upright. His entrance pulsed and discharged streams of semen and Patrick lapped it right up, loving the taste of himself. He burrowed with the tip of his tongue; he lashed Oliver's tender opening and rivulets of spunk and saliva streamed down Oliver's thighs and dripped onto his tight little sac.

Patrick reached around to grab Oliver's straining, leaking cock. He pulled at it hard as he let Oliver push back and back until his plump, beautiful arse was nearly suffocating him. When he had his tongue right in there, thrusting into tight, giving muscle, Oliver came.

He shrieked. His hole fluttered, ran white, and sucked on Patrick's tongue. His whole body convulsed, shook for seconds on end until, without warning, he fell down and Patrick just about caught him before he hit the ground.

Patrick had cleaned him up, uncuffed him and laid him on his bed covered with a blanket by the time Oliver stirred. He had never fucked anyone into unconsciousness before and had anxiously considered calling an ambulance, until he had checked Oliver's breathing and pulse and found them present and strong, if a touch erratic.

He stood looking at Oliver for a while and when he had decided the student wasn't going to die, he smirked to himself with egotistical glee at making Oliver pass out in pleasure.

Oliver's thick lashes fluttered. His eyes opened and he

blinked myopically at Patrick. 'I didn't dream you,' he said, his voice hoarse.

'No,' replied Patrick, folding his meaty arms.

Oliver's gaze dropped down his hard body, in his combat pants and half-undone shirt. Patrick basked in Oliver's obvious interest, his cock thickening.

'Where are my glasses?' Oliver said. 'I need to see you better.'

Patrick obediently passed them from the bedside table. Oliver put them on, propping himself up on one elbow. Then he gave Patrick a long, searching look from head to toe, lingering on his washboard abs and the bulge in his pants. His sensual little mouth formed a soft "oh" of something resembling astonishment.

Patrick smiled indulgently. He was in no rush to go home. 'See anything you like?'

Oliver bit his lip and nodded.

Patrick unfastened his pants. His prick sprang loose eagerly. 'This?'

Oliver squirmed on the bed. His hand moved busily beneath the blanket. 'Yes.'

'Think you can handle it again?'

'Oh yes.'

'Very well.' Patrick stripped quickly. He pulled the blanket back and found Oliver wanking under it. The student moaned softly as Patrick joined him on the bed. Limbs entwined; they kissed. Patrick felt that jolt again when their lips met and it spurred him on to clasp Oliver's slender body close to his. To hold him the way he didn't usually hold anyone.

For a moment, he pulled away to look down into Oliver's flushed face with his pink, parted lips and lashes trembling over closed eyes.

He thought of the money he had received for this job and decided to give it back to Harry. This time would be for free, and all the subsequent times after it.

## Stud Poker
## by Landon Dixon

I didn't wake up with a hangover; I woke up with a raging hard-on.

I blinked my eyes, tried to focus. Oh yeah, I'd crashed at my buddy's place after an all-night poker session. I hadn't been drinking much, but Todd had insisted that I sleep what little I had off at his place. He let me use the bedroom belonging to his roommate, who was supposedly away on business.

I was lying on the guy's bed in just my Jockeys, cock stiff as an ace-high straight, tenting the thin underwear like a tall stack of chips. Todd's roommate, Kurt, was sitting on the edge of the bed, very much at home, his warm, brown hand riding my bare, muscled thigh.

'What the …!' I gargled in shock, scrambling up onto my elbows.

'Morning, Brent,' Kurt said.

'Uh, yeah … Morning,' I replied, glancing from my wood to the guy's manicured hand, back again. There seemed to be a direct relationship between the two. My face lit up like a Budweiser sign and what little spit I had evaporated in my open mouth. I was more than a bit confused.

Kurt smiled, his mouth warm and wet and friendly. Then he moved his left hand further up the charged, peach-fuzzed skin on my left thigh, causing my cock to jump right out of its foreskin.

I didn't have a clue what to do. I'd never had a sexual encounter with anyone in my entire 18-year life, and I didn't know how to react. But my dick sure did; it went so hard it vibrated, as Kurt moved his delicate hand up and down my thigh, caressing me.

The guy was dressed in only a pair of tight, white Jockeys himself, his smooth, lean, golden-brown body blazing at me, his blond hair tousled, green eyes soft and sensitive and staring into my wide, blue ones. He was a year older than me, but that's about all I knew about the guy. But I was finding out more and more as the seconds dragged by on crutches – about him, and myself.

'Have a good sleep?' he asked, soft palm gliding back and forth on my rigid upper leg.

'G-good s-sleep,' I gulped, goosebumps flaring up all over my pale, overexposed body.

Kurt looked down at my raging dong, his long fingers digging in and squeezing my tensed thigh muscles. 'Maybe ready to play a little – stud poker?'

I swallowed my Adam's apple, my elbows shaking beyond my control. I could smell the sweet, tangy scent of the guy, feel the incredible heat of him through his supple hand, see the long, hard outline of his own arousal in his briefs.

His hand moved higher, and the polished tips of his fingers brushed against the shaft of my cotton-stretched cock. I jerked like a total amateur, which is exactly what I was. His smooth fingers slid up and over my throbbing erection, tightening around my shaft. I gasped for air, my body flooding with a wicked, sensual heat, my head going dizzy. Kurt gently rubbed my pulsing cock, sparking my latent desire into open flame.

Then he suddenly released my prick and gripped the

elasticised band of my underwear, said, 'It's your first time, huh, Brent?'

It was more of a statement than a question. I nodded, more to what he was doing than in response to what he'd said. Kurt pulled down.

I arched my bum off the bed and he skinned my Jockeys off, and we both gazed at my crotch, at my straining, naked, needful hard-on, my bare want revealed. Kurt grasped my rod skin on skin, and I yelped, 'Fuck!'

'Later – if we play our cards right,' he breathed, his warm, sure fingers sliding up and down my pulsating shaft, swirling over my bloated hood.

My whole body shook so hard I thought I'd walk the bed right out of the room. Time stood still, all the air sucked out of the room, leaving a breathless vacuum of raw sexual sensation, highlighting the hellacious honesty of another man's soft hand on my hard cock for the very first time.

I could barely control myself, prick swollen to enormous size and sensitivity under the beautiful man's tender stroking. And when he pulled me up and lowered his head and flicked his wet, kitten-pink tongue at my purple hood, I just about jack-rabbited right off the bed with excitement.

I clung to the damp sheets with my damp hands, desperately trying to hold myself in check, the tingling in my body and balls already redlining. Breath hissed out of my flared nostrils like steam out of a ruptured pipe, as I watched Kurt twirl his slippery tongue all around my mushroomed cap, felt the incredible wet-hot friction right down to my outstretched toes.

The guy pumped my dong with a circled thumb and forefinger while he slapped my cockhead around with his tongue, licking up a sticky gob of oozing precome and smacking his lips with satisfaction.

I thrust my rigid body upwards, pressing my cap into Kurt's moist tongue and lips, urging him to quench my agonizing sexual thirst. And he opened his mouth up and took me inside.

'Jesus!' I hissed, spasming.

Kurt sealed his lips around my knob and sucked, tugging on my cock, pulling me fully over the line, over to his side, the man knowing just what another man needs and wants. He locked his jade eyes onto mine and lowered his blond head, his lips sliding down my bumpy shaft, consuming me. I pushed upwards, jamming my engorged meat into the wet cauldron of his mouth, hardly able to believe what was happening, and never wanting it to end.

He inhaled three-quarters of my cock, and then pulled slowly back up again. I groaned with sensual pleasure. He fingered my furry balls while he bobbed up and down on my numb-hard dick, sending me sailing. The guy wet-vacced my cock with a wicked suction, his tongue wagging across the boiling underside of my shaft, his teeth barely scraping the surface of my lust.

I howled, 'Fuck, Kurt, I'm gonna –' But it was already too late. Muscles locked up all over my body and my cock unloaded, ecstasy exploding inside me, sizzling sperm spurting out of my slit and dousing Kurt's throat.

I jumped around like I'd won the biggest pot of my life, blown away by the blistering intensity of my very first man-on-man orgasm. My head spun off into orbit and my body went molten, hips bucking with every furious blast of my joy.

Kurt squeezed my balls with his hand and milked my cock with his mouth, his throat working hard and fast, as I came for what seemed forever. Until at last I collapsed back down onto the wet sheets, drained and deranged, and he opened his mouth and released my spent dick in a gush of warm saliva and come.

'You rest, big boy,' he said, wiping his mouth, patting my heaving chest. 'We'll deal ourselves another hand a little later.'

I stared blindly up at the ceiling and sucked hot air into my billowing lungs, body and soul as limp as a guy whose bluff's just been called. I could barely comprehend what had happened, only knowing that I'd liked it; no, loved it. And wanted more.

Strength slowly flowed back into my wasted body. I climbed back up onto my elbows and scanned the room – no Kurt. I rolled off the bed and staggered to my feet, stiff-legged it out of the bedroom and down the hall, bobbing cock leading the parade.

I skidded to a stop at the open bathroom door. There was Kurt, flush out of the steamy shower, his long, tapered, lightly muscled back to me, towelling himself off, his bubble-butt filling my eyes, and cock. I moved on instinct, dick rising higher and guiding me. I walked up to the man's golden, round-mounded bum and sank my fingers into the deliciously pliable flesh.

He straightened up and looked over his shoulder at me and my desire. 'Hmm, I see someone's ready to play some more,' he said, smiling a dazzling smile.

I kneaded his taut buttocks, revelling in the hot, ripe feel of the man's ass, the tip of my prick brushing his bronze skin. He groaned and leant back into me, turning his head so that our mouths met, easily and naturally.

I kept a hand on his ass, clutching at his damp, blond hair with the other, while I fed on his soft, full lips with a ravenous, pent-up appetite. He darted his tongue into my mouth and bumped it into my tongue, and I surged with tingling heat. We swirled our slimy stickers together over and over, my cock firing steel-hard against the burning, velvet skin of the man's ass.

Kurt spun around in my arms and hugged me tight, pressing his naked body against mine, his hard cock into my cock. I quivered with delight, our tongues urgently entwining. He clawed at the bunched muscles around my shoulders, then latched onto my plump butt cheeks and squeezed them, slapped them. As I got the full, erotic feel of a hot, hard man in my arms for the first time.

Eventually, he broke away from my mouth, bent his head down and licked at my nipples, teasing the pink buds harder and higher, filling me with a weird, wonderful buzzing sensation. And when he hooked a hand under a bouncing pec and captured a rigid nipple in his mouth and sucked on it, bit into it, I cried out with dizzy joy.

I grasped his shoulders and spun him around, pushing him forward, up against the sink. 'I'm gonna fuck you!' I hissed, all-knowing and macho-like.

He looked at me in the mirror and grinned, wagging his sexy behind like a red flag at this bull. Then he popped the medicine cabinet open and plucked out a bottle of lube and a condom, handing them to me with the question, 'You sure you can handle these stakes?'

I nodded, not trusting my voice. I fumbled the cap off the lube and rubbed the stuff all over the length of my pipe. Before I figured out that the condom went on first. Kurt didn't laugh, though. He just gripped the white enamel edges of the sink and swished his bottom from side to side, patiently waiting for me to come and get my first luscious piece of man ass.

Despite the tremble in my fingers, I somehow fought the condom open and on, then re-lubed my pole. Then I slid a pair of slick fingers in between Kurt's swollen cheeks and rubbed the man's crack. And I must've rubbed him the right way too, because he groaned, his buttocks shuddering.

I greased him up to the extreme, not at all sure where the dividing line between pain and pleasure lay. My fingers slid all the way under him until I touched his hard-packed sack. He jerked, and I dug deeper, curling my arm up between his legs and grabbing onto his twitching cock on the other side.

'Yes!' he moaned, knuckles matching the enamel.

I started stroking the guy – pulling on another man's hard cock! – his smooth, cut prick jumping in my slippery hand. It was an awesome rush of eroticism, and power. I stroked and stroked his cock, squeezed his bulbous cap, juggled his shaven balls, turning him hot and me inferno.

Finally, he bumped his ass back, reminding me of what I'd boasted to do. It was time to show him my hand, or fold. I let go of his dick and gripped mine, steering my shiny cap in between his cheeks, pressing up against his pucker.

'Fuck me! Fuck my ass, big boy!' he shouted, thrusting back, bending my cock almost in two, before swallowing my hood with his asshole.

I was inside him – inside a man! My legs buckled with the enormity of it all. Kurt pushed back even further, my cock plunging into his asshole. I grasped his slim waist and watched in awe as his butt kissed up against my body.

I swallowed hard and hesitantly moved my hips, and my cock slid back and forth inside his gripping butthole. I was fucking a man! My blood and balls boiled with the outrageous, superheated sensation, with the breathtaking sight of my cock churning that golden boy's glory hole.

It was way too much for this inexperienced butt-fucker to handle. 'I'm gonna come, Kurt!' I bleated.

He instantly slammed back against me, popping my cock out of his winking pink asshole, padded cheeks sending me flying against the wall. Then he quickly scooped up the lube and another condom, grabbed me by the erection, and towed me back into the bedroom. And before I could wrap my head around the insanity, I was flat on my back across the bed, Kurt standing alongside, gripping my legs against his body, his gleaming, latexed cock probing at my dripping opening.

'We're going to cash in our chips together, stud,' he purred. 'One big *jack*-pot.'

I felt his cap push against my resisting pucker, then pop through, inside me. I moaned like a wounded animal, a strange, full-up feeling filling my heated body, as Kurt dove his cock deep into my chute.

'Oh Jesus, yes, fuck me!' I cried, tearing at the sheets, the man's long, hard cock plugging my aching need to the hilt.

He rocked back and forth, rocking my body and world, pistoning his big cock in my tight sex-hole, stretching my chute. I shivered with glee, my own benumbed hard-on flapping in rhythm to Kurt's thrusting. It was the most wild, wonderful feeling in the world – getting ass-hammered by another man – and I revelled in it, rolled in the dirt of it, rejoicing at the bolts of sexual electricity that ripped through me each and every time my lover pumped my flaming ass.

'Jerk yourself off, Brent!' he hollered, smacking against my rippling cheeks faster and faster. His nails bit into the meaty flesh of my thighs as he reamed me, fervently ploughing both of us to the point of no return.

I grabbed my jumping erection and frantically fisted. My cock jerked in my hand, and before I even felt the towering waves of ecstasy crash through my body, hot jizz leapt out of my slit and splashed down onto my chest.

Kurt pumped even faster, the sight and scent of come sending him into a frenzy, his pile-driving prick splitting me in two. Then he tore his cock out of my swollen butthole, flung off his condom and sprayed his own orgasm all over me. Warm spunk showered down on my chest and stomach and hand and cock, mixing with my jizz, both of us jacking burst after burst of semen out of our rock-hard cocks, my violated ass gaping its emptiness.

Todd found the two of us in each other's arms, glued together by our mutual lust, basking in the warm afterglow of our high stakes sex games. 'So you went all-in on Brent, huh, Kurt?' my buddy said, grinning.

My lover gave my lips a lick, grinned right back. 'Yes, thanks for convincing him to stay the night. It made things quite a bit easier. Although, it really didn't take much to convince this stud that poke-him is a lot more fun than po-ker.'

They laughed, while I sighed the contented, manly sigh of the busted virgin.

# Spangle
## by Alcamia Payne

Spangle's giving up smoking and it isn't easy, not easy at all, he thinks as he nurses his macchiato and his fingers dance impatiently around his china mug. Cigarettes have given him a sex voice; deep, husky, and provocative. Shit, he can milk guys with just a whisper and a fondle.

Spangle rubs the large crucifix around his neck. Smoking, huh; well, it isn't gonna be easy and he reckons he'll need all the help he can get as he fingers the packet of smokes in his pocket. Max said go cold turkey or keep just three smokes for like an emotional prop; Izzie said find a diversion, Spangle, you know, something harmless to take your mind off it, something cool like a hobby.

'Do you mind getting your legs off that chair?' Izzie says, her lips forming a line of disapproval as she flourishes her notepad. 'This is a café, Spangle, you know you can't sit here all day without ordering something.'

'Order something.' Spangle puts an unlit cigarette between his teeth. 'OK, doll –' Leaning forward, he fixes her with dreamboat eyes, the colour of Caribbean larimar. 'Order me that guy sitting over there in the corner, the guy in the suit, the handsome Italian kid.'

Izzie, the attraction burning like torchlight in her dark gaze, puts her hands on her hips and licks her dewy, frosted lips. Everyone lusts over Spangle and he is kind of cool for an older gay guy. Chicks dig his roughhouse style, his beanpole thin legs squeezed into red leather pants, his black leather jerkin open down to his flat belly, showing his pierced nipples and his slim, agile dancer's hips.

'Shit, Spangle, Faldo's a stockbroker and he works in the city. What's he gonna see in you, you hippie misfit, you?' She grins, pokes him in the ribs and leans forward as, chewing her gum, she mouths, 'You dirty old man.'

Spangle sexes her out with one of his stares while he twirls his nipple ring around in his fingers and ponders – well, hot damn, if this isn't the diversion he's been searching for. His eyes like blue magnets zone in on Faldo and Spangle wriggles his saucy hips lower in the chair as he tries to accommodate the mammoth erection which is forcing his zip and generating a pleasant glowing pain in his groin. Spangle's into orgasm in a big way, and that's a kind of addiction too. He has a super-sensitive dick and an erection feels like cool gloves smoothing his body and invisible fingers tickling his balls. He enjoys it immensely; in fact, he likes it so much he often puts himself in situations just so he can zone out on a dirty five minutes of imaginary foreplay.

Faldo slouches indolently in his fine Italian suit, his long legs stretched out and his hands in his pockets as he reads a newspaper. His fingers play nervously with his long strands of dark hair; the motions of his super-sexy fingers toying with the slicked-back waves creating such a tousled mess he now looks like a bohemian artist. He's also loosened his fancy cuffs and a frosting of dark, curly hair shows on Umbrian tanned wrists.

Spangle peers at the curly wrist hair, imagining what might be under the rest of the designer linen and at that precise moment Faldo glances up and his eyes, which are the colour of coal and capable of deep and meaningful emotion, stare into Spangle's. An electrical jolt surfs through Spangle, making the tips of his nipples and cock tingle and his heart beat like a jungle drum.

Spangle is chewing on his bottom lip, contemplating jerking off on this cool diversion, when Faldo gets to his feet and goes into the john at the back of the café. Feeling like a fish on a piece of fishing line, Spangle follows him.

When he opens the door, Faldo is standing with his hands on the hand basin. He's taken off his tie and unbuttoned the top three buttons of his shirt and he's staring in the mirror. When he turns around he stuffs his hands in his pockets. He looks damned sexy with his shirt askew and his slick hair now flopping across his forehead.

'Hey,' Spangle says. 'I'm Spangle.'

'What kind of fucking name's that?' Faldo says meanly.

Man, he seems like an unfriendly bastard, but the fact is Spangle scares Faldo in a sexual way. Faldo has been sitting in the Blo Jo Café for weeks because he's dead crazy over the blond guy but afraid of how if he got his hands on that pale streak of heaven he'd be able to control his hot Italian passion. Well, today he's got the jolt he needed because he's just had the heave-ho at work and all that anger's been transmuted into the need for a good, hard fuck. God, he's got to be crazy to be so turned on by a guy at least ten years older than he is. After all, Spangle's got a face like he's been through a meat mincer and he towers over Faldo at about six foot five. Despite dressing really weird in all those ripped tops and black leather jerkins with the jangling chains and metal, though, he's super sexy and hot, hot, hot in a down and dirty way. Faldo licks his lips. Hey, it might be kind of cool to have some bleached blond rough; he's only ever fucked clean banker types with Smeg designer kitchens and Mercedes.

'Hey, loosen up.' Spangle's sexy foreplay voice drips all over Faldo, the melodious, husky tones tweaking Faldo's groin and stroking his balls and making him think of those chains and leather and a dark room somewhere, where Faldo can be brainwashed out of thinking about stocks and shares and profit margins.

'Fuck me,' Faldo says, grabbing Spangle's jerkin and propelling him into a cubicle.

Spangle's brooding lips are very close and Faldo pokes out his tongue and touches them. Spangle hums like someone just plugged him into the national grid as he neatly traps Faldo's tongue in his teeth and accosts it with long, slow strokes and sucks, said organ slithering and tangling with Faldo's until the kisses become full-throttle passion. Faldo slides his hand up Spangle's bony back and begins stroking. He moans as Spangle thrusts against him, his fine shirt hanging open to reveal a toned body with carefully sculpted muscles and smooth skin. His hand is on Spangle's crotch, his fist opening and closing in heart-like, pumping movements.

Sweet, real sweet, Spangle thinks.

'Man, fuck me,' Faldo groans.

He's an expert at zips, buttons, and attachments, and after a couple of passionate embraces he tugs down Faldo's pants, getting to work next on the fancy boxers.

Faldo sits down hard on the john, his eyes rolling back in wonderment as he groans, 'Fuck me,' again, under his breath. It makes Spangle feel all warm and mellow inside. Dropping to his knees Spangle, jerks down Faldo's designer underwear and eases out his cock, caressing it thoughtfully before pinching it between his thumb and forefinger, and then lowering his mouth to lick at it experimentally. It tastes great and he traps it between his fleshy lips, easing it inside the warm, velvet cavity and beginning to work it; circling the meaty pole with his tongue, scraping tender flesh with his neat white teeth until Faldo arches his back and moans saucy Italian expletives. Boy, Spangle thinks, rich cock, delicately garnished with expensive continental cologne, tastes great in relation to nicotine.

Faldo lies on the bed, staring upwards and wondering why anyone would paint the entire constellation of Cassiopeia on their ceiling. He kind of expects Spangle to come in with a joint; instead, he's leaning against the bathroom door, butt naked and with a boner so huge, it's unreal. Spangle has spent ages staring in the mirror and gazing closely at his craggy face as he remembers sucking Faldo off in the john.

Earlier Faldo had stripped off and taken a shower. Spangle's seen some great bodies at the strip club but Faldo's in a league of his own. Naked, he's like a Greek God and the kind of guy who could easily do sexy commercials and make a bomb at it. Spangle had licked his lips and a giant fist clenched around his heart as he watched the suds foaming down Faldo's body. Hell, it was difficult to resist that perfect, tight, clenched butt. The shower cubicle was really small, but Spangle stepped in behind him and then he lathered up lots of soap and before Faldo could object he soaped him all over. Slick sex was fun, with their cocks nosing together, hot and wet, and their tight nipples super-sensitive from a shot of ice-cold water, thanks to the badly functioning, coughing and spluttering plumbing system.

Now, Faldo's eyes shine in the darkness and Spangle experiences a slow, crawling sensation like icy fingers up his spine, which lifts his balls and tightens his apparatus. Only half an hour ago Spangle had been pinned to the bed and that muscular body with the tight, punchy butt was driving into his arse in slow, measured movements. Spangle was fast beginning to forget about cigarettes; actually, he was developing an even worse craving. Smoothing his thumb down over his concave stomach, a slow and rather macabre smile curls his lip. Well, what the hell. Spangle strolls into the bedroom.

Faldo is staring at the Fender guitar in the corner. All of Spangle's apartment is papered in pictures of rock groups.

'Say, you famous or something ...? That your bass guitar?'

'Christ, you sure as hell ask a lot of questions, but, yep, that's my guitar.' Spangle suffers a clenching in his belly. He knows he's about to tell a cracking lie and he can only blame his bad nerves on the lack of nicotine. The trouble is Spangle's always been a dreamer and he always wanted to be a rock star. The fact of the matter is he bought the Fender from a flea market, he can't actually play a note, and the Fender doesn't work.

Spangle's crotch is itching and, when he looks down, a tiny, spangled sequin nestles between his balls, shining like a distant star in that constellation of Cassiopeia. He flips it covertly with his thumbnail. 'Well, man, sure, in my day, I was kinda well known; now I do mostly session stuff for some of the mega bands.'

Faldo's gaze is riveted on Spangle's crotch. 'How come I haven't heard of you, then?'

Spangle shoots him a loaded glance. 'Maybe because when we were riding back, and you were straddling my Vespa and getting all sweaty, you told me you were only into classical stuff. You don't even like rock, remember? You're into Handel and Puccini. Besides everyone knows me as Spangle and I don't play as Spangle any more.'

'What do you play as, then?' Faldo's grin is loaded with innuendo as he twists Spangle's nipple ring and, flicking out his tongue, experimentally licks the hard nub. 'I have to say, Spangle, you sure don't seem like a bass player. Bass players are tall guys with stooped shoulders and they're built like Polish weightlifters.'

'What the fuck, Faldo? I wish you'd shut up.' Spangle wriggles up the bed and, putting his feet on the headboard, lets Faldo play with his balls and cock. Soon, he's soaring as his tool slides in and out of Faldo's mouth. Faldo eats him like he eats his favourite pastrami sandwich, nice and slow, with nibbles and long, gustatory pauses, and definitely not like Spangle, who swallows everything down real quick. Hey, he loves this guy. Hell, Spangle ponders, I'm in trouble.

As it turns out, giving up cigarettes has been the easy part. Spangle's living dangerously, lying to Faldo, but what can he do? He's in love and life has suddenly become very complicated indeed. Once, the club had been enough. Now, though, Faldo's talking about bringing all his stuff over and moving in. Shit, the worry's making Spangle think about cigarettes like crazy until he realises he likes sex with Faldo more.

Big Billy's sitting slouched in a chair in the dressing room, nursing a scotch and rolling his large gold rings around his meaty fingers. He's frowning from beneath his long, dark eyebrows. 'You gotta be crazy. What's all this shit, Spangle? I sure as hell don't know what's got into you. One moment you're surfing the stratosphere, the next you're talking about resigning.'

'Yeah,' Spangle says, as he mulls over the million and one different ways he can break the news to Faldo that actually he's not a rock star and he's never stroked a chord in his life. Sure, he's famous, so famous he's done a full frontal spread for a national magazine, but he's famous for a kinky strip show involving lots of spangles and nothing much else – and he certainly ain't no rock star. Spangle's belly aches with the threat of impending loss. Shit, he can't imagine a sophisticate who spends his time fine dining and going to the opera digging spangles.

Spangle raises a cynical eyebrow as Billy exhales plumes of blue cigar smoke, then, opening a packet of designer spangles, he shakes them out. Boy, that Japanese guy's something else. He's custom made some cool spangles which are larger than the average. It's all part of the new act which should give the randy guys in the front row a bigger memento to snatch as they jam dollar bills into the little pouch Spangle keeps around his waist.

'You ain't gonna really quit on me are you, Spangle? Why you wanna do that? How about I offer you another two hundred, how about that? I can't afford to lose a proposition like you.'

Spangle pauses as he tugs back his bush of blond hair and fastens it with an elastic band. Sex and money, the two greatest temptations on earth, what a joke. His heart gives a funny lurch. He fancies a nicer pad where the plumbing works. He's been saving like hell and soon he can afford the rent on a better place, perhaps closer to Faldo's classy joint. He feels like he's being tugged this way and that, by material temptation on the one hand and love temptation on the other.

'Well hell.' Billy claps a hand on his shoulder. 'I never did this before, but I'll give you a month. Just say you'll think about it.'

'I'll think about it.' Spangle smirks.

That night the new spangles keep dropping off. It's an

art form getting spangles to stick just tight enough that they don't come loose when he's dancing, but are easy enough for the punter to snatch off during a hip gyration. Billy suggests using some glue and now, dammit, the spangles won't budge. Shit, what the hell's Faldo going to think? He reckons an itsy-bitsy spangle's weird enough, let alone two the size of dimes and shaped like twin suns which are artfully adhering to Spangle's balls. If it wasn't so serious it'd be funny. What's more, the dissolving solution hasn't done any good at all and his dick's so pink it looks like a strawberry popsicle.

Spangle sits in the dark outside his apartment, straddling his Vespa and staring up at the window. What the hell's he going to tell Faldo, when Faldo's so hot and horny? Shit, he'll have to make an excuse.

As it happens, Faldo is as usual stretched out on the bed with the window open and the lights off, his body bathed in blue and red striped neon.

When Spangle comes in, he showers, changes into a pair of training pants and sits down on the bed, his body startling white and his hair long and loose around his shoulders. Faldo stares at him and Spangle takes his hand and, kissing it, begins sliding his fingers into his mouth, caressing them so that Faldo closes his eyes, moans, and clutches his dick.

'I love you like crazy, Faldo.'

'Good, I'm glad about that.' Faldo's hands move gently back and forth beneath his boxers.' Faldo has a way with his cock and he likes to milk it. Spangle shivers; he's reaching the point of no return.

'Hey, lover.' He falls on Faldo, fondling him with his hands. 'I'm feeling really tired tonight, I reckon I'm coming down with something. Mind if we just sleep?'

'Hell, no.' Faldo smiles as they spoon together in the

darkness.

Spangle jerks Faldo off while he watches his seduction in the antique mirror which stands on the floor at the side of the bed. He walks his fingers up and down the lusty tuberosity while he kisses Faldo's neck and grinds his spangle-encrusted crotch into Faldo's tense, muscular butt.

Spangle still can't loosen the damn spangles and it's the same old story the following night and the night after that. He can tell Faldo's getting angry, as his brows are perpetually drawn down over his sexy, dark eyes and he keeps asking Spangle awkward questions. Spangle's heart's tripping as he watches Faldo, in a loose T-shirt and chinos, frying eggs. He looks so cool, so sexy.

'You sure you're not telling me something? I mean, I'm looking for work if that's the problem? It's not as if I'm lying around,' Faldo says.

Spangle glances approvingly over the apartment, which Faldo has done up. He's painted the walls and cleaned the kitchen. The place has never looked better. 'Hell, what the fuck?' he exclaims. 'That don't mean shit. So take your time, find the right job.'

'Well, what is it then?' Faldo comes over, draping his arms around Spangle's neck. 'Maybe you're losing interest in me, perhaps that's it? Maybe you don't like having me around 24/7?' Then, pouting, he does a slow strip tease, easing off his T-shirt and throwing it on the floor as his gaze smoulders, then wriggling his pants zipper down far enough to show a tempting square of pink, engorged flesh before stripping off the chinos completely. Spangle shudders; the craving for Faldo's toned flesh is driving him crazy.

'Hey, no offence,' Spangle exclaims, backing rapidly

towards the door. 'But I don't have time for this. I just popped in, that's all; I gotta be out to meet one of the guys to see about some studio time.'

Faldo's mouth turns down in consternation. 'Hey, Spangle, what the fuck's the matter with you? Man, you can't be in that much of a hurry.' His lips curl up in a snarl. 'How can you do this to me? I told you how my other boyfriend lied to me and how I hate that stuff, Spangle. Oh, I get it, loud and clear.' Faldo snatches his T-shirt off the floor. 'You've got someone else, haven't you?' His eyes are blazing as he backs Spangle up against the door. 'Well, fuck you. I know you've been hiding something for ages. Who is he? Who's the bastard?'

'There isn't anyone,' Spangle says, spreading his hands in placatory fashion, his whole body in overdrive. 'Come here, lover.' He tries to tousle Faldo's hair, but Faldo shakes his hand off like an angry dog. 'You know how it is, I explained. I have to rehearse late, that's all. You know I'm always up late, burning the midnight oil.'

'I hate you.' Faldo says, pushing his semi-naked body closer, his face in Spangle's, very close so their mouths are almost touching. 'Why the shit won't you let me come with you sometimes? You ashamed of me or something? No, No.' He puts his head in his hands. 'You two timing bastard, you're afraid I'll see him, this, this – other guy. Shit, you rockers are all the same.' Faldo's trembling with rage. 'I should have seen the signs with you not wanting to strip off and come straight to bed. That's it, huh? I get it; you were always having to shower his jism off before you came to bed in case I guessed. God, what do you take me for, some asshole? Older guys, who wants them? Thinking the sands of time are running out, fucking anyone you can get your hands on.' He jabs Spangle juicily in the groin. 'Well, buster, I got news for you, the game's up. I'm out of here.'

The roughhouse is only arousing Spangle and he feels comfortably tingly. There's a kind of surrender in his limpid blue gaze. Relaxing back against the wall, his heart steps down to a metronomic beat. Tick-tock. Wow, he loves Faldo and he loves him more than ever when he's wild and passionate like this.

Spangle bursts out laughing. He can't help it; his hard-on is aching and the spangles are itching like hell. In a second his belly hurts so much he's bent double. Faldo blazes as he pummels Spangle.

'Shit, man, and now you got the nerve to make fun of me.' He's panting heavily when he eventually finishes, skin slicked with perspiration, his wild hair messier than ever. God, he looks good as he tries rather unsuccessfully to wrestle back into his chinos, leaning over with his muscular butt presented. 'Go to hell, Spangle.'

Spangle watches him, his heart contracting and relaxing. Faldo can be so fiery, so emotional.

Spangle steps forward and grabs him around the waist. 'Hold it right there, I got something to say. I gotta come clean.' Spangle blows gently in his ear. 'I think perhaps I ought to take you to bed and show you something.'

'You'll be lucky.' Faldo says. 'Get out of my face.'

Spangle wrestles him onto the bed, trailing his sensual lips down Faldo's dark line of belly hair to those balls and that incredible weapon poised in its nest of crisp pubic hair. Faldo is pinned to the bed and he's stopped struggling as Spangle pushes up his T-shirt and licks his nipples, teasing the buds into pleasurable hardness.

'You needn't think you can get round me this way,' Faldo moans as Spangle slithers down the bed and then, 'oh, what the fuck.' He whimpers as Spangle begins teasing his lips and thrusting his tongue deep into his mouth. 'What the fuck, why do I love you so much?'

Spangle reckons he might not have heard properly. His cock's now in orgasmic overdrive as the spangles tingle and Faldo's own tool brushes his thigh. Come to think of it, he hadn't realised before quite how erotic spangles feel.

He puts his hand on Faldo's erection and squeezes it, making a claw of his hand and expecting to see a flicker of pain in Faldo's eyes. Instead, Faldo's stare is mocking as his mouth gapes open and his lips quiver. Maybe he's a masochist? Spangle hopes so. He wets his lips as he floats slowly out to sea on a tide of lust.

'You'll have to do better than that if you want me to forgive you. You'll have to take me with you tonight, huh?' Faldo grunts.

'Yeah, maybe you're right. Perhaps it's about time you saw what I do,' Spangle replies, his voice low and husky as he takes the blindfold off the bedside table. Faldo likes a bit of kink, but this time Spangle has an idea. Faldo lies with his mouth slightly open as Spangle strips and then peers at his spangled cock. The spangles feel like they might be beginning to work loose and, boy, it's kinky. He kind of likes the weird sensation, the prickling, the burn. It's like a weird form of sadomasochistic torture.

Faldo's licking his lips in anticipation of the game.

Sometimes Spangle teases him with a banana simply to get him in the mood; however, today he just snuggles up to Faldo's mouth and lets Faldo's sinuous tongue lick his wet tip. Boy, it feels good. Shit, he ought to have put his cock ring on because he'll want to come real quick after so much abstention. Leaning forward, he lets Faldo devour his pumping tool, those velvet Italian lips feeling like erotic heaven. But shit, Faldo's licking his balls and he seems to have found a spangle and now the tip of his tongue is digging around and nibbling as a vertical line forms between his eyes.

'Hey, what's this?'

'Body art,' Spangle says.

'Shit body art.' Faldo rips off the blindfold, his eyes deep, lusty pools. 'Man, they're spangles; that's sure weird for a macho guy like you.' He blinks. 'But wow, kind of kinky.' Pouting Faldo then does a naughty thing: he bites Spangle very gently and tries to slide his tongue under the spangle to loosen it. Shit! Spangle clenches his fist; it feels so good, he wants to shoot.

'Ah,' he groans. 'Hell.'

'Man, I knew you were kinky but not that kinky.'

Perhaps, Spangle speculates, he's gonna get away with it after all, but hey, you can't lie to your lover can you? Taking a deep breath he says, 'Fuck it, I'm a dirty rotten sinner because I lied to you. The thing is I ain't no rock star, Faldo. I'm Spangle, I'm a stripper. I do this show, not nancy stuff, real macho stuff, you know – cages and a bit of dirty, hog-tying bondage.'

For a moment Faldo's gaze darkens then he says, 'Man, I hate you,' flipping the spangle rather painfully and starting a curiously electrifying quiver up Spangle's spine. 'We get close and next you lie to me. Why would you do that, Spangle?'

Spangle shrugs. 'I dunno. I mean, a guy who does a kinky show with spangles dating a rich Italian stockbroker. It sounds kind of weird, a bit off base.'

'A failed, out of work stockbroker, you mean.' Faldo grins.

Spangle shrugs, and sighs. 'So I suppose this means it's over?'

Faldo traces a line down Spangle's belly, circling his balls before hesitating just a moment to flip the spangle and move deliciously in rotating movements over Spangle's cockhead. Faldo puts his finger in his mouth and, providing some lubrication, continues to circle until Spangle feels a supercharged glow. Next he puts his nail under the spangle and, flipping it viciously, sends a ricochet, a mega stab of pleasure, straight into Spangle's groin, which is kind of cool.

'I kinda had these custom spangles made by this Japanese guy but they wouldn't stick, so Billy suggested this glue. Now the bastards won't come off and I didn't want you to see, Faldo, didn't want you to guess.'

Faldo licks his lips and his eyes become moist like he might be going to laugh.

'Know something?' He winks. 'It looks kind of sexy for a guy to be shining around his crotch like the constellation of Cassiopeia.'

Spangle's holding his breath; he can't believe it as Faldo's vice-like grip tightens and he pulls Spangle's meaty stem nearer to his mouth. The sensual Italian lips tremble; simply a feather of a kiss and then the lips are slippery teasing deep throat pleasure.

'This could be fun,' Faldo says to Spangle. 'You got the handcuffs?'

Spangle gets the handcuffs. 'So Faldo, you're not disappointed I'm not some hotshot rock star?'

'Sure, I'm mad as hell.' He shrugs, spreading Spangle out and licking his lips as he straddles those groovy narrow hips. 'But I'm kinda glad. Rock stars have a bullshit attitude.'

Faldo's tongue dances over Spangle's skin, leaving fiery trails. Faldo's a cool lover and he takes his time to lick and flick. When he gets to a spangle, he stops. 'So shit, man, you gonna let me come?'

'You're so good at innuendo,' Spangle says huskily.

'I didn't mean that, idiot.' Faldo eases the tip of his tongue under the spangle, and then, placing his whole mouth over it, he begins to work things.

Boy, sex never felt this good, Spangle muses, as his fists clench and his cock feels like it's on fire from all this nibbling and sucking. 'Yeah, yeah.' He groans. 'Harder.' Faldo eats him slowly; he slides the swollen length into his mouth and the caressing velvet walls massage Spangle in a silken glove while fingers continue to tease miniature suns.

Spangle erupts like Vesuvius, greedy and thrusting, and afterwards Faldo kisses him with deep, thrusting kisses. Boy, does it get better than this?

Spangle sits down in the dressing room at his battered old table and, switching on the light, he stares into the mirror. Opening the box, he begins to apply the spangles. He's thinking it's going to be explosive when Faldo licks and nibbles them off later on. When he comes out of the dressing room, Faldo's rehearsing and stalking across the stage. He looks good with his glistening pecs and in the Roman gladiatorial outfit Billy dreamt up. Hell, he always knew Faldo would make one hell of a stripper.

Faldo's hands slither across Spangle's firm, sequin-encrusted torso. 'Hey, you put them on! I was rather hoping you'd let me do that.' He's being teasing as his lips come closer and Spangle's hands wander down over Faldo's almost naked, leather-encased butt.

You know something?' Spangle kisses Faldo and their lips and tongues suck and caress. 'Dammit, I reckon I beat that cigarette craving; I reckon I'm cured.' He glances at the packet with the three cigarettes on the table. 'And this addiction sure beats nicotine.'

# The Wrong Side of the Glass
## by Josephine Myles

*Hic ... Hic ... HIC!*

Bugger! This always happens when I have a night out drinking and someone makes me laugh.

I stumble out the side door of the pub into the alleyway. Fresh air will probably do me some good. Shame that's in short supply, what with the heat wave we've been having. At least it's quiet and secluded out here, so I should get a chance to pull myself back together before braving the crowds again. I gasp in a couple of lungfuls of humid, cigarette-scented air before the next spasm hits me.

*Hic.*

I decide to hold my breath. Over the years I've tried all the zany cures helpful friends have suggested – including eating peanut butter, standing on my head, and screaming (not all at once, I hasten to add) – but I know oxygen deprivation is the only sure-fire cure. Unfortunately, I always end up practically suffocating myself before the bloody things stop. Might be OK if I had a kink for auto-erotic asphyxiation, but I've always thought that was a mug's game. Can't even bear to wear a tie, which is probably why I'm still working as a barman at the grand old age of 23.

I take a deep breath and clamp my lips shut. I even pinch my nostrils closed, because it's so easy to give in to the temptation to cheat. Fully immersed in my cure, I look around and wonder if it's just a figment of my oxygen-starved brain, or if that really is the most drop-dead gorgeous man I've ever seen leaning back against the wall. He has a shaved head, muscles bursting out all over the place, and the kind of cheekbones you could cut yourself on. He's wearing a black T-shirt with the sleeves and collar cut off, so it hangs low under each arm, and those jeans leave very little to the imagination. I'm so distracted, my body lets rip with a mortifyingly loud *hic!*

He stares at me, eyebrows raised, and puffs out a perfect smoke ring before flicking the ash from his cigarette. My face heats as I give a little wave and try to calm my breathing.

'Hi there. *Hic*. Name's Pete.'

As conversational openings go, it's not the smoothest. But he takes another drag and gives me a bemused smile, so I'm encouraged to carry on.

'This is the point – *hic* – where you're meant to tell me your infall – *hic* – ible hiccup cure. Come on, everyone's got at least – *hic* – one. It'd better not be the giving you a blowjob – *hic* – one, because I've tried that and no matter how much jizz I – *hic* – swallow, it never works.'

That's when I remember I'm not at one of my usual haunts, but have in fact been drinking with straight friends in a normal pub – the main reason I got so wasted in the first place. I say a "normal" pub, but it isn't really. Marie's a goth and her favourite boozer is full of big men in biker jackets drinking real ale with belligerent names like Headbanger. It's plain cruel, inviting me somewhere with such delicious man candy, but all off limits. I needed all those poorly mixed cocktails just to relax.

I wonder if getting your head kicked in by an enraged straight bloke cures hiccups.

Fortunately, he doesn't seem to be bothered by my clumsy chat-up line. He just gives me an assessing gaze over his cigarette. I try to look serious in return, but it's bloody difficult when my over-active diaphragm keeps sabotaging my efforts. In the end I settle for medically fascinating, with a side order of drunken charm. I try to tone down the sultriness, but it's bloody impossible when he looks that good.

'You should try drinking from the wrong side of a glass of water,' he says in a deep, rumbling voice. 'You know, bend over and drink it upside down.'

I want to roll my eyes, but that would be rude and probably take me one step closer to that head kicking I so narrowly avoided earlier. 'No, tried that one. *Hic*. It never works. Just get water every – *hic* – where.'

'Might suit you,' he says, raising an eyebrow. I catch it then. That brief flick of his eyes down to my chest and back up again. Oho! He's definitely picturing me in a wet T-shirt. I should try it out, test if there's anything more than a purely intellectual interest there. I mean, I might not be built like him, but I've got nothing to be ashamed of. I work out enough to have pretty good definition.

'Here you go,' he says, handing me the glass that was sitting on the ledge beside him.

'Water?' I ask. Somehow I'd have expected something stronger, more macho. A pint of Skull Crusher ale, for instance.

He just raises his eyebrows and takes another long drag on his ciggie before stubbing it out on the bricks.

'What can I say? My body is a temple.'

Oh yeah, and one I'd like to worship at. Not so sure the smoking goes with the purity thing, but maybe it's like the devotional incense.

'It certainly looks divine,' I say, looking up through

133

my eyelashes, insanely proud of managing to force out one whole sentence between hiccups. Then I let rip with a really big one that surprises us both and echoes down the alleyway. They could probably hear that one inside, even over the blare of Korn on the jukebox.

Trying to hide my blushes, I duck down and attempt to drink from the wrong side of the glass. It makes my head spin and I stumble, but a solid arm comes out to steady me. I cling on to it gratefully, take a couple of huge gulps and then straighten up with a mouthful of water.

*Hic.*

It floods down my chin, dripping onto my chest. A cool rivulet runs over my nipple and it instantly stands to attention. Something else is starting to stand to attention as well. Huh, who would have thought it? Must be the effect of that strong arm still wrapped around my body. That and the smell of him. All fresh sweat and musky maleness. I watch his eyes grow darker as he takes in the wet fabric clinging to my pecs. Maybe I should try the blowjob line again. I think we've now established that he definitely isn't straight.

'Starving your body of oxygen should help,' he says. There's a predatory growl to his tone, and I find myself praying I'm not about to fall victim to a serial killer with a weakness for hiccupping twinks.

Fortunately, when his hands close in around me, it's my waist he goes for, not my neck. He does a top notch job of trying to suffocate me with his tongue, kissing me so thoroughly I forget to breathe. His stubble rasps against my chin and I'm smothered in a smoky taste sensation: sharp and sour and oh-so-good.

'Mmm, you taste sweet,' he mumbles, before diving back in again and fucking my mouth with his tongue. He might not be a drinker, but he certainly seems to appreciate the flavour of a Screaming Orgasm made with way too much cheap vodka.

*Hic!*

I burst out in a fit of nervous sniggering. He couldn't possibly find this sexy, could he? But then again, maybe he has a kink for hiccups because he's looking even more interested now.

'You know,' he says, his voice a low rumble that passes right through me, 'I once read that digital rectal massage is the only sure way to cure hiccups.'

Never would I have thought something so clinical sounding could send all my blood rushing to my dick. 'I'm happy to be your – hic – guinea pig.'

He steers me down to the end of the alley where there's a large wheelie bin – fortunately it doesn't smell too awful as it's being used for empty bottles rather than food waste. Behind the bin there's a small area out of sight of everyone. Unless they should choose to walk up here, of course. The idea of being caught sends a delicious thrill shivering down my spine.

'Do you taste this sweet all over?' he asks, before thrusting his tongue back inside my mouth for another kiss so aggressive, I swear I'm gonna lose some fillings.

'Only one way to find – *hic* – out,' I say, the next time he lets me snatch a breath. And a hiccup.

He pushes me back against the wall, gives me another hiccup-punctuated kiss, and sinks to his knees. He makes quick work of my fly, and before I can hiccup again my cock is boinging out of my pants and hitting him in the face. He doesn't seem to mind, and makes this low, guttural sound that almost makes me come there and then. He shoves my jeans and briefs down around my knees and starts nuzzling into my crotch. I think he might have forgotten about the rectal massage bit, which is a shame.

Where's a hiccup when you need one?

*Hic!*

Yeah, there we go. I pull on one of his hands and manage to get it up to my face. He swallows my dick at the same moment I suck two of his fingers in. They taste salty and a teeny bit tarry, but it's a good, masculine flavour. I whimper around his fingers, trying to give them the same attention he's giving my cock. He's doing something with the tip of his tongue that feels divine, pressing it into my slit on the top of every stroke. The next hiccup makes me buck and I thrust right into his throat. He doesn't gag, just takes it all in his stride. I feel like I'm in capable hands. Thinking of hands …

Once his fingers are thoroughly coated in saliva, I pull them out of my mouth and move his hand to where I want it. He did promise, after all. He looks up at me. It's hard to tell the colour of his eyes under the orangey glow of the security lamp, but they're big and dark and looking at me like he wants to eat me up. Which he kind of is, already.

I hiccup again, a half-hearted one, like my body wants to stop. *Not now,* I scream at my diaphragm. *Keep going! He's nearly there!*

And then his finger pushes against my hole and I forget to breathe. He tortures me like that a while, just a gentle pressure on the rim, all the time humming around my cock and looking up at me with his eyes all crinkled in amusement.

'I want my cure! You – *hic* – promised!'

He smiles around my dick. I can feel his lips tighten and shiver with anticipation. I'm so bloody close now. And then his thick finger pushes in past that tight ring of muscle. It hurts in the best possible way. There's a sound coming out of me, all needy and turned on, but at least I'm not hiccupping any more. And then he moves inside

136

me, brushing that spot that makes my knees turn to jelly, and my orgasm rushes out of me. My body's wracked by a much more enjoyable set of spasms as I hold his head down and pump his throat full of come.

I lean back against the wall, waiting for the world to return to normal. He gets to his feet and leans in to give me a bruising kiss I can taste myself on. God, if he keeps that up I'll be good to go again in a minute. Actually, that might not be such a bad idea, considering the size of the bulge in his jeans. I give it an experimental grope. Yep, Christmas has definitely come early this year, and I've been a very good boy indeed.

'You know,' I say, 'I'm pretty ticklish, and if you make me laugh I might well get another fit of hiccups.'

'OK, point noted.' He gives me a puzzled look and searches out my lips again. I have to turn my head to evade him.

'No, wait! I'm bound to get them even worse the second time. A finger wouldn't be nearly thick or long enough to effect a complete cure.' I squeeze his dick for emphasis.

I see the moment he catches on, the mischief transforming his face. His eyes glint with lust as his fingers wiggle their way into my armpits. I squirm and start to snigger.

*Hic!*

Yes!

# The Stable Hand
## by Jasmine Benedict

Victor Hatridge quivered. He was not, of course, the breed of man to permit such feeble things, but there it was. Climbing like a creeper, winding its tendrils round his spine, a shiver thrilled through him, despite his prime position at the fireside. Leaning with his elbow on the grand, marble mantelpiece, Victor bowed his head and cocked it aside, gazing intently into the rampant flames that frolicked behind the grate while feigning an eligible bachelor of a laugh.

Hattie Sherritt was chirping nonsense as usual. Every rich man's heir in the county proclaimed her voice to be that of a nightingale – and admittedly it was so – but a nightingale would surely have had more substance to express with its nightly effusions than this little darling ever could. Presently, she was chirruping the praises of her dressmaker; an excellent man who, to quote her flowery diction, was "an absolute artiste with silk and chiffon". Victor had no interest in silk or chiffon. His mind instead wandered to the fancy of plain, coarse linen stowed hurriedly behind an abrasive waistband of heavy tweed. Furthermore, to the hands that had stowed it there. Rough, weathered hands, skilful hands, strong hands left trembling weakly, out of character …

Victor quivered once more. He exhaled a slow, steady breath and kicked the heel of his riding boot against the

138

hearthstone. It simply would not do for Miss Sherritt to perceive how he quailed and presume herself the cause. Glancing up begrudgingly, he felt thankful that the rubescence of firelight in his cheeks should mask more telling a flush. He smiled at Hattie simply to perpetuate the illusion of his attention being at her disposal, but all the while his eyes desired to look past her; to peer beyond the halo of her fire-kissed ringlets, and to seek a sight far more enchanting to his eyes.

Happily, just as Hattie had thrown herself into a rapturous overture on the wonders of Iroquois beadwork, Victor was afforded the opportunity he so desired. Entering the parlour, a clumsy serving maid caught her tray on the handle of the door, sending a jarring clatter through the pleasant hum of after-dinner conversation that had hitherto filled the room. Victor fought hard not to smile as the chance to look past Hattie thus arose, levelling instead a masterly scowl at the servant and sending her scurrying about her business with her head ducked low. Secretly, he wished to guffaw in the face of her habitual awkwardness. But alas, Victor Hatridge had not breath enough to spare.

Halfway across the room by now, the figure that had caught his eye upon entering – the tall, broad figure that had caused him to tremble so helplessly just moments before – was cutting out a definite path towards him. Victor allowed himself no more than a heartbeat to drink in the appearance of that figure, but even such a fleeting observation was enough to stir his vitals to painstaking attention. Strapping, strong, but out of his depth, sidling uneasily between the clusters of future lords and ladies, Eli Brown appeared as incongruous in the lavishly furnished room as might a stag stumbling in off the moors. His dark tweed breeches were, Victor noticed, tucked studiously into his thick woollen stockings, lacking the habitual lopsidedness that tended to mark his attire under less formal circumstance. His upturned shirt collar had likewise been coaxed out of its accustomed unevenness, straightened on the right where his bristled jaw line tended to rest while he shod the manor's horses, flattening the stiff tab of fabric against his broadly muscled shoulder. The simple scrap of a cravat beneath was neatly knotted and – just to complete the air of effort made – his dark, unruly hair gave the definite impression of having been run through with anxious fingers before he had entered the room.

Having granted himself this brief inspection of Eli Brown, Victor dutifully returned his attentions to Hattie, finding as he did so that she had grown increasingly objectionable by contrast. Still she twittered on, but now her senseless rambling, mildly annoying before, was enough to enrage his every sensibility. Still she inclined her pretty little head, making certain that the firelight caught her dollish cheek as flatteringly as possible, but now the contrived absurdity of it made Victor wish to stomp out those flames and her vanity with them. Patiently, though, he pandered to her pointlessness, taking great amusement in the fact that he secretly thought her a fool while she presumed he adored her. How delicious her comeuppance would have been had she discovered that, while she batted her lashes and envisaged herself the future Mrs Hatridge, her intended beau was entertaining thoughts of errant passion with a rugged stable hand.

''Scuse me, sir.' The stable boy in question arrived at Victor's side with fortuitous timing, speaking out in that broad, northern drawl of his in the very same moment that a memory of gruff, male pleasure yelped like agony flashed through his master's mind. Victor steeled himself against both the imagined sound of Eli's whimpered ecstasy and the reality of his coarse, uncultured tone. Somehow that thick accent made everything he uttered seem an invitation to infinite sin.

'Yes, man? What is it?' Victor too spoke in the manner typical of him; a brusque, commanding baritone that masked whatever sentiment he felt towards the intrusive underling. Fractiously, he eyed Eli as though impatient for his departure, but they both knew what the master truly desired.

'Sorry, sir,' Eli apologised with a genuine air of hesitancy about him. 'It's just ... One of the horses, sir. She's had a tumble in the paddock. I think you'd best come see, sir.'

'Has she, indeed?' Victor took a moment of haughty contemplation to best admire Eli's countenance in that moment, from the way he toyed irritably with one rolled-up shirt sleeve, to the faintly belligerent aspect that had sharpened his hazel eyes. No matter how many times they engaged in these little tête-à-têtes of excuse and acceptance, Victor always managed to leave Eli ruffled; hinting at the untruth of his words, though only the two of them knew it, and forcing him to linger for longer than was necessary in the lavish rooms that so discomfited him. All on purpose, of course. There was nothing quite so divine in the world as that rough-edged man of the country in a dour, ill-tempered state.

'Do excuse me, Miss Sherritt.' Victor's voice came out a little more gravelled than was common of him, the thought of what might follow irrepressibly intoxicating.

'Of course,' piped Hattie sombrely. 'Poor horsey ...' But Victor strode away before she had the chance to utter more.

The walk to the stables commenced in total silence and

remained so for its entirety. Victor marched off in front, as was his manner when strolling anywhere with anyone, leaving Eli to bring up the rear, a few steps removed. Victor could hear the younger man's riding boots crunching out his lengthy gait on the frost-bitten path behind, and knew that Eli could easily have passed him on those long, muscular legs of his. He would never attempt to do so, though. Until they were shut away somewhere secret, Eli never seemed willing to transcend their respective roles of servant and master, no matter how irksome he found them.

Nearing the long, low, red brick out-building that housed the manor's horses, Victor slowed and performed a sprightly half-pirouette while still in motion, striding backward and casting the deeply serious Eli a rakish smile through the frozen cloud of his breath.

'Lead on, man,' he ordered, since it had struck him that he had no idea which one of his half-a-dozen horses had allegedly taken a tumble in the paddock. The stable hand responded with a nod of brisk courtesy, bowing his head while his previously well-checked steps elongated, carrying him past Victor with ease.

Completing his theatrical turn, the master observed his earthy companion cutting out ahead, and admired such a welcome hind view of him with quiet delight. Eli's dark breeches fitted him impeccably well, tightening to his firm, muscular buttocks on the left and right, and left and right, with each purposeful step he took. Set in motion too, the hunting crop that hung from his belt beat a gentle tap, tap, tap against his brawny thigh as he strode, while his strong, bare forearms – as if they knew – swung just enough to accentuate the hypnotic shifting of his haunches. It struck Victor that Eli's weathered skin appeared immune to the bitter chill of the January air.

Mercilessly, that same frigid atmosphere nipped the master's own nose, cheeks and knuckles to painful rawness, and the thought of yet more delicate parts of his anatomy being exposed to the same gnawing cold caused his core muscles to contract with aghast anticipation.

Following Eli into the stable block, Victor found himself engulfed by the pungent aroma of leather and straw; that, along with the relative darkness of the sparsely windowed space, causing a certain sensation of having wandered out of one world and into another. This world was Eli's world; his clothes and hair forever held the memory of it in their familiar, earthen scent. Even when he dared to venture across the divide into Victor's lush universe, Eli always brought that faint fragrance with him, and it was a fragrance that had long since become fundamentally entwined with arousal in the depths of Victor's subconscious mind. Even now, as he strode along the stony aisle between the rows of penned-in horses, Victor's body was subject to the effects of that ingrained reaction. He could feel the invigorating thump of his heartbeat quicken against his ribcage, the rush of eager lifeblood course mechanically southward and, yes – as he watched Eli pause to unbolt the final stall on the left – the slow but certain stiffening of his cock.

Eli slipped through the stable's heavy half-door like a thief, turning once within and, at last, allowing his brooding gaze to meet directly with his master's. The look that he levelled at Victor was one of belligerent command, and its recipient fancied him a stubborn, dark stallion, steaming at the nostrils and refusing to be moved. Victor smiled at the image. He moved towards the door and propped his lean body against the frame while smiling still. Reclining there, lazily, he made no further move, merely watching as the effects of said smile grew apparent in the demeanour of his tightly wound companion. Eli's heavy-set jaw line flinched with taut annoyance, his powerful hands balling into exasperated fists at his sides. He heaved out a furious snort of a breath, but that just reinforced the comical equine metaphor in Victor's mind.

'I see no horse here,' the master observed, with enough of haughty amusement in his tone to make Eli visibly seethe. Standing there, bruised and belittled, Victor half expected the poor, frustrated thing to paw the ground and make a charge. And, as it turned out, he was not entirely wrong.

'You forget your place, boy.' Victor twisted on his heel and made a grand act of departing. 'I do not appreciate having my time wasted.' But scarce a step had been ventured before his performance was brought to a close.

With force enough to wind him, the entrapment of Eli's arms flung themselves about Victor's athletic frame from behind. Covetously, the stable hand snatched his departing master backward, dragging him into the stall – the door kicked closed to pen them in – and hauling his stumbling body impossibly near.

'*I* forget *my* place?' That gruff, rumbling drawl threatened like thunder in Victor's ear. Lazily, his captor's hips slunk forward, an impatient erection foisted into the sculpted flesh of one male buttock. 'Nay, sir … Rather *you* forget *yours*.'

'And where …?' The master had intended to frame a snooty, if breathless, rebuttal, but the unuttered words were stolen from his tongue as a hand unhooked the button of his breeches with a short, sharp tug. Victor's breath took a hiccup in his throat and he felt the heat of laughter lick the shell of his frozen ear.

'And where …?' Eli echoed tauntingly, his surly voice, indeed, bearing the cadence of a semi-quaver's mirth. Victor's lips parted once more to frame an answer, but a sharp nip of teeth to his earlobe addled his mind and left eloquence for dead.

Reeling with desire, the unseated master could muster no form of defence as his conqueror forced a grasping hand down the front of his breeches. Could only whimper and teeter back against the solid wall of a body behind him, as an unyielding fist fell closed about – and took a rough-palmed drag along – his aching shaft.

It seemed, contrary to Victor's suspicions, that Eli's flesh did feel the cold. Indeed, his icy grasp upon the heat of a throbbing erection was akin to that of some spectral being. Stern and unforgiving, that glacial hand secured itself about the base of Victor's startled cock, thwarting his anatomy's inbred desire to recoil from the cold and driving his blood to an angry throbbing at the summit. Victor gritted his teeth. He screwed his eyes shut and let his skull fall back against a thick-set shoulder. Somewhere in his mind, he had the thought that he should have fought it, but he knew this surrender was all he had ever truly desired.

'Do go on …' Eli mouthed those words as hot as coals against Victor's goosebumped throat, punctuating them with a slick sweep of tongue above the skittish pulse that galloped there. 'Sir.' That title was affixed more as a jibe than a mark of esteem by now, but Victor found the disrespect of it delicious.

'And – where is my place?' he managed at last, in a voice of crumbling stone, swallowing heavily as Eli's thick hand flexed upon his cock and drew its way languorously up, bunching silken folds of skin about the testy head, a thumb swept over the raw, slick nerves of it, before smoothing down the length of him again.

'Where indeed?' The rebuttal left Eli's throat in a wolfish snarl of insolence, and Victor fancied himself a pheasant, flailing in the jaws of the beast. Shaken into stupefied submission, he was discarded, a knee thrust in behind his own to buckle his legs. Dazed, he collapsed to the floor, a jellied heap at his servant's feet, yelping with muddled elation cum anguish at how cruelly his sensitive cock had been torn from Eli's grasp. Hunched upon all fours, he felt it bob free, yanked from his breeches amidst the fall, and as the wintry air breathed agony upon it, he bowed his head and panted his defeat.

'Aye.' The triumphant crow of Eli's victory was paired with a boorish boot to Victor's rear. 'That is your place, sir,' came hissed as a dangerous promise, and Victor knew well that it was true.

The stable hand tarried, his forearm lazing on his upraised knee; Victor felt it in the shifting of weight stacked against him. Bowing his fair head in deference, impatience, frustration, delirium – something – he sought to push back; sought to plead another boot. Seeking would not get him far, though. Eli was not a merciful lover. Too many years spent serving Victor's kind while they treated him with less respect than their foxhounds had seen to that.

Forcing himself to wait, the lowly master stole a backward glance beneath his own panting body, glimpsing the purpled gleam of his swollen manhood. Wetting his lips, he resisted the urge to reach for it; to palm it and work some solace through its jilted, floundering length. Eli must have read his mind – more likely the flinch of temptation in a biceps or shoulder muscle – for out of the stark, frustrating nothingness there came a mighty crack.

Leather. The flat, narrow tongue of a finely crafted hunting crop on the taut tweed of breeches pulled tight to a vulnerable rump. The sound hit first. Victor started. He watched as his cock jerked and mithered mid-air, like an agitated snake's head. For a breathless, bewildered moment, the oddly rigid sway of it hypnotised him – and then came the shock-delayed impact of the blow.

Victor's eyes screwed closed, his entire body cringing as the sting of the lash caught belatedly, like a fire in his flesh. His hands formed numb fists on the dull prick of straw and he squirmed as his body caught light, a rapturous hiss drawn in through gritted teeth and exhaled on a deep-throated moan. The pleasure-flame tore through fresh nerves, expanding, while the core of it contracted, goosebumps tightening on his skin. His aching balls bunched up in sympathy. His teeth caught his lip and his eyes fluttered open. Through his own trembling lashes, he watched as a fresh pearl of moisture emerged at his cock's angry tip, hanging there, daintily suspended, quivering timidly and then slipping away to paint a jutting blade of straw. He could smell it …

'Aye, sir liked that, di'n't 'e?' Eli slipped into the thickest vernacular, caring not for the airs and graces forced upon him by the world beyond these stalls. Dealing a parting shove, his foot descended. Victor caught the faint scuffle of hands unhooking coarse fabric and swallowed on a lump of impatient desire. Blinking past his own braced thighs, he watched as Eli's knees came folding down to the floor. A hand seized the waistband of his breeches, freezing fingers curled beneath it, and in a single, urgent tug, his rump was bare. A second yank worked his breeches to the ground, and one pliant leg was coerced from the thick slump of fabric, though it snagged where it was tucked below the knee, beneath his tight-laced riding boot. Somewhere amidst the tussle, the graze of a brawny thigh, still clothed, plied its way between the nudity of Victor's, forcing them wider apart, his bare knee scraping over the ruts of cobbled stone through the strange, satin prickle of trampled straw.

Victor whimpered mindlessly. A palming hand splayed across the shiver of his left haunch and his back arced like a cat's as he was spread open. Solid and stiff, yet smooth as finest velvet, Eli's splendid cock slid forth along the seam of his vulnerable body. The slick, searing head kissed his entrance. The puckered skin there rippled with expectance and dismay. Breathing hard, he braced for it, his own arousal tightening to a maddening degree. His head swooned and his heart raced, pressure pounded in his ears. He steeled himself for the blunt, mind-bending breach of being taken ... But, alas, the intrusion never came.

Sliding beyond instead, his lover's thick shaft too caressed the testy flesh in the valley of his roughly parted flanks, gliding on between until the warm, doughy weight of Eli's balls was nestled like a curling, snuggling kitten against his rear. Victor slackened, mewling, settling back, sinking into the tenderness; the slow, smooth slide and the yielding, almost embrace-like halt so far departed from the fierceness he had expected. Eli snarled his approval at Victor's pliancy, however, and the master was reminded that a tiger, not a kitten, held him captive in its claws. As if to affirm the fact, a slow, bewildering tickle spider-crept its way up Victor's naked inner thigh and, choking on his own breath, he realised it was the popper of that riding crop, somehow quite forgotten. Some part of him wished to fear it, another to goad it into action; he was torn between evading the pain and embracing the pleasure it might bring him. Higher, higher still, that threatening tab of supple leather grazed the goosebumps of his hair-flecked skin, reaching the delicate juncture where lean, athletic thigh met defenceless, softly hanging nether-flesh, and dallying there, tracing idly between.

'Best make it easy on yerself, sir.' Eli's ominous words came to Victor through a blind, bewildered stupor. Still, he understood them; rose on trembling hands and pushed back, striving urgently, for his own sake, to obey. Studiously, he worked his naked haunches back and forth along the kingly length of Eli's lounging cock, hearing him mutter some low oath as he watched himself be rump-fucked, sandwiched lazily in the writhing, snug divide.

Victor felt a speck of burning moisture brand the small of his back, and he knew, with a leap of his heart, that it would not be long. Sure enough, Eli's stern hand left his rump. It flattened instead to his rolling small. Forcing him down to his elbows once more, it bowed his spine profoundly and smeared that fresh-spent glob of humid arousal between them.

Sliding back now of its own desirous volition, Eli's cock once more butted the entrance of Victor's body, pressing at it this time, smooth and slickened with the fruits of the master's efforts to ease the passage for himself. Hunched to the floor, Victor screwed his eyes shut and clenched his jaw, his breath withheld as Eli's need-glossed head slipped in. Pressing, pressing still, it plied him open, fighting through the fierce resistance of an impossible, giddying fit. Somewhere, through the scream of overstretched muscle and agonised unity, the delicate tickle of leather drew slowly up the underside of Victor's weeping cock. Crying out, he slackened just enough for Eli's humbling length to breach another impossible inch. That last, exquisite inch that took him sinking right to home.

Eli folded forward. Victor struggled to hold his weight, that broad, solid body heaving into his in the closest they came to embrace.

'Aye ...' The hilt-deep stable hand murmured deliriously to himself. 'Aye, sir ...' He rubbed his stubbled cheek against the shirt-clad strain of Victor's shoulder. 'Whatever would Miss Sherritt say if she 'appened ter see yer now?'

'Fuck me ...' Victor astonished himself with his own, outspoken demand, the thought of this act – this exquisite, forbidden, unthinkable, animal act – being watched by the wide, fawning eyes of that vain, naive being damn near doing him in.

Forgetting himself in that liberating thought, Victor was startled, cursing fiercely as the tongue of Eli's crop came out of nowhere, swiping sharply up at his slackened, sloping belly, where his shirt hung loose, exposing his skin to the lash. Flinching, arching away from the sting, Victor skewered himself ever deeper onto Eli. In gruff, growling symphony, both men revelled in the almost unbearable cram of it, the stable hand blowing out a long, slow breath that brought his broad, bent bodyweight sinking more heavily in.

'You forget yer place, sir,' the deep-seated servant taunted hoarsely. 'I shall decide when I should fuck yer ...' But before his words were even fully uttered, he was.

Being fucked by Eli was to ride a wild stallion through a forest at night, or rather to hang on to fistfuls of mane and let it tear off as it liked while hanging on for precious life. All was a breathtaking blur. There was pain, as of tree branches whipping one's flesh. There was pleasure, euphoria, heart-thumping, panting adrenaline, coursing thickly, damn near bursting from one's veins. There was rhythm; the hammering madness of rump on the back of the runaway steed. There was pounding connection, unstoppable motion, ceaseless fury, and, above all else, one thing: there was the petrifying thrill of realising that one was helpless, at the mercy of a beast far superior in power to oneself. It was freedom, abandon, unequalled, unrivalled, unutterable rapture to fuck – nay; be fucked by – this man. This wayward, unprejudiced, wild, classless steed of a man, born to servitude and labour, yet so powerful, so grand …

Hastened away on that thundering mount of fevered imagination, Victor keened as he was driven from the edge. He might have uttered Eli's name somewhere amidst the frenzy. Might have proclaimed him a prince or a god. He could not tell. Thrown from the fictitious beast, he went hurtling to earth and landed heavily, a winded, quivering, brainless heap of a thing. Slumped upon the reality of straw, he felt it stick against his heaving stomach, coated in the hot mess of his own still-firing seed. Trapped beneath the weight of both his own spent body and Eli's – still thrusting, now pounding him into the ground – his cock convulsed and jerked and throbbed. Gasping for breath, Victor rode it, lying motionless and crushed while his lover still strove toward completion, fucking the last, aching spasms of all that he had from his shattered, passive body.

Throwing forth one final, growling shunt of his hips, Eli burst, and Victor's exhausted body gave a dull, euphoric thrill at the hot, heady rush of his lover's climax surging within him. Boneless with sated exhaustion, the stable hand quivered and slumped completely, swathing his master's much leaner body to an infinite degree. In the midst of a sky-high, almost prayer-like murmur, his damp lips happened upon the fluster of Victor's cheek, mouthing an unheard word against the clammy, cooling skin there. A word that felt rather chest-stirringly like a kiss …

'Victor?'

The moment was broken. A sharp jolt went through them, still perfectly joined. That damned overrated birdsong of a voice had come from far too close; a stark reminder of the world that went on turning just outside.

'Victor … Is that you?' Hattie Sherritt was drawing ever nearer, and for a long, rash moment her intended beau considered just letting her find him – letting her find *them* – here like this. Eli was scrambling away, though; he was prising himself from the snug fit of Victor's body. He whimpered and Victor could tell that his lip had been bitten to deaden the sound. Victor somehow found that he no longer cared, however, and as the exquisite, burning fullness of Eli's waning cock slipped free from his body, he bemoaned a sullen protest unreservedly, worrying not.

'Sir …' That word was hissed in the hushed, insistent tones of a man flushed with panic; a man almost tumbling from his shaky, weakened knees as he fumbled with his breeches and his cock.

Victor heaved a sigh. He supposed that he must arise and go. He did not want to, but he supposed that the world, as ever, would make it so. Lifting his wearied weight onto infantile hands and knees, he rose unsteadily and sank back, squatting on his naked haunches.

'Victor? Victor, do come out if that is you,' Hattie's chirping voice insisted, and Victor glanced down sadly at his sated cock, now wilting in his lap.

'Sir!' Eli's fretful voice urged him once more, and Victor felt those strong but scared hands each seize a fistful of his half-discarded breeches. Hurriedly, they wrestled his free leg back into the crumpled garment, the limb hauled out from under him with clumsied haste. Tipped forth once more, Victor rested in a tranquil, bowed position, sighing wearily as the tiresome, coarse

152

concealment of fabric was hastened up over his rump.

''Ere, put yerself away, sir,' Eli fretted, clearly baffled and a little afraid at his master's apparent abandoning of his senses. Victor had never seen a thing more clearly, though. He wished to stay here with Eli for ever. He did not wish to return to that false, judgemental world. He did not wish to go.

Rising to his knees once more, Victor gave a languid stretch as Eli's strong but fearful arms came round his body, his hands now seeking for and striving to stow away his master's lolling cock. Victor reclined in those arms; he rested, quite calm, on that heaving, heart-thumped chest, and as Eli fixed the button of his breeches with a fumble, he gave a smile and languidly turned his head.

Eli was going to speak; the master saw it and captured his parted lips in the silence of an obstinate, fiery kiss. The stable hand wavered at first, stunned no doubt by the curious display of post-coital affection ... But then he softened beautifully, loosening into it and gingerly kissing back.

Victor was first to break free, though the taste of that hesitant tongue was a nectar to die for. Wetting his lips, he savoured it while seeking Eli's baffled gaze and seizing the wrist of the shuddering hand that still endeavoured to set him straight. Keeping it from stowing his shirt beneath his breeches, Victor urged the anxious palm to press and curl against his crotch, watching as shades of mistrust, astonishment and – yes – of doubtful ecstasy arose in Eli's eyes, at the murmuring of an order in a most collected voice:

'Steady that hand, boy. Let her come.'

# Boys of Summer
## by Michael Bracken

I don't think any of us expected that Saturday to turn out the way it did, but with temperatures in the triple digits, a cooler filled with Shiner Bock in the bed of Delbert's Chevy Silverado, and the swimming hole all to ourselves, I don't see how it could have turned out any different.

The swimming hole is a wide spot in Carter Creek, on private property a mile and a half up a two-rut road from a Farm to Market. Delbert had a key to the gate, having done odd jobs for Old Man Carter, and it was his idea to be shed of town for the afternoon. He talked Gary and me into joining him when he offered to provide the beer and the ice to keep it cold.

We didn't plan ahead all that well and, when Delbert pulled his truck to a stop under the towering oak that shaded the near side of the swimming hole, we realised that not a one of us had brought swimming trunks and we only had towels because Delbert kept a supply in his tool box to use as rags when he was working away from the house.

That didn't slow us down none. We just stripped down to our altogether and let our peckers flap in the wind as we waded into the cool, spring-fed creek. The ground on the near side, where we'd left the truck, was pretty near flat, sloping gradually into the water, and we could easily walk into the creek until we were about waist-deep before the bottom dropped away. Of course, by then, cold-water shrinkage had affected us all and none of our peckers were flapping.

The creek's more than about ten feet deep on the far side, where it butts up against a rock wall about twenty feet high, and if we were of a mind to we could climb about five feet up that cliff and cannonball into the water below. Delbert, being the most adventurous of us, did it three times before an accidental belly flop had him yelping in pain and had Gary and me laughing our butts off. After that we just swam and floated and shot the breeze.

All three of us had farmer's tans – leather brown faces, red necks, and dark arms from our fingertips to the leading edge of our T-shirt sleeves. Except for various amounts of body hair, everything else about us was albino white and when any one of us headed to the Silverado for beer we looked like ghosts emerging from the water.

After a few beers we started horsing around. Delbert dunked Gary. Gary dunked me. I dunked Gary again. And pretty soon our excitement counteracted the cold-water shrinkage we'd experienced earlier.

We had been friends for ever, the three of us, and we'd paired off a few times over the years, but that afternoon was the first time the three of us ever did anything together.

It started when Delbert and me spotted Gary floating on his back with his eyes closed and his pecker standing at full attention. Now Gary's not what you'd call a longhorn, but his erect pecker cast a nice enough shadow nonetheless.

Delbert nudged me and then dove under the water. He came up on the other side of Gary and gabbed a fistful of Gary's pecker just as I came up under Gary and supported his ass to prevent him from sinking or pulling away.

'What're you dreamin' about, some skinny-ass city boy down in Austin?'

Gary protested at first, but when Delbert started pistoning his fist up and down the length of Gary's pecker shaft, the swollen purple mushroom cap popping out the top of Delbert's fist like a one-eyed prairie dog, Gary quit struggling and was soon moving his hips in rhythm to Delbert's fist pumps.

I couldn't help myself. While Delbert jerked off Gary, my own pecker grew stiff as a fence post, and I knew I was going to have to do something to relieve the pressure. Though tempted to reach under the water and take matters into my own hands, I continued supporting Gary's weight until he came.

He erupted like a geyser, jetting a long, thin stream of come straight up in the air that rained down on his chest. Delbert released his grip on Gary's pecker and I pushed him away, sending him floating toward deep water as he tried to catch his breath and keep from sinking at the same time.

I walked out of the water to Delbert's Silverado, my erect pecker leading the way, and grabbed a fresh bottle of Shiner Bock from the cooler resting on the open tailgate.

'You're going to get a sunburn on that thing,' Delbert called.

'Not if I find a dark place to stick it,' I called back. I popped open the beer and took a long swallow.

'We ain't got any lube,' Gary protested as he left the water to join me.

'In my glove box, dumb ass,' Delbert shouted from the creek. 'You think I go anywhere without it?'

After Gary opened his own Shiner Bock, he walked

around the truck to the passenger side and retrieved a half-used tube of lube from the glove box. He tossed it to me. I fumbled a one-handed catch because the tube was hot, and it dropped onto the tailgate.

'We ain't going to be using this any time soon,' I said as I picked up the lube with two fingers and dropped it into the beer cooler. 'Use this now, it'll be like dipping your pecker in French fry grease.'

Then I spread one of Delbert's crusty towels on the tailgate so I wouldn't burn my bare ass and hiked myself onto it. My pecker was still jutting up from my crotch like some kind of petrified snake, and Gary noticed it when he returned to my side.

'What are you planning to do with that?' he asked.

'I was planning to do you,' I said, 'until I burned my fingers on that tube of lube you threw at me.'

'Maybe there's something we can do about it while we're waiting for the lube to chill.'

'You suggesting what I think you're suggesting?'

Gary took a swallow of Shiner Bock and then wrapped his lips around my swollen pecker head. The combination of his hot lips and the cold beer made my eyes open wide.

'Jesus, Gary,' I said to the back of his head. 'Where'n hell did you ever get the idea to do that?'

I didn't expect a response and I didn't get one. Gary was too busy giving my pecker head a tongue-lashing to say much of anything.

He wrapped one hand around my stiff shaft and began pumping up and down as he continued licking my pecker head. I set my beer aside and pressed my fingers against the back of his head. The bristly hair from his recent flattop jabbed my fingers like tiny cactus needles as I pressed down, encouraging Gary to take more than just my pecker head into his mouth.

He had to swallow the Shiner to do that, and he must have, because he slowly took in my entire length. I soon felt his warm breath against my damp crotch hair, when Gary drew his face away from my crotch. His beer-wet lips slid smoothly up my pecker shaft. Then they slid back down. As I set my own beer aside, I glanced out at the creek. Delbert was watching us and, from the way the water was moving in front of him, I suspected he had taken matters into his own hands.

I leant back and braced myself in the pickup bed as Gary face-fucked me. As far as I could see through the branches of the oak, there wasn't a cloud in the pale blue sky. But I only had a moment to notice. As my climax approached, I closed my eyes and felt my entire body begin to tense. Gary must have noticed because he reached between my thighs and grabbed my nut sack.

I couldn't restrain myself, even if I'd wanted to, and I erupted in Gary's mouth, providing him with a come chaser to his beer. My pecker spasmed several times and Gary swallowed every drop of my come.

My pecker quickly withered and Gary pulled away. He retrieved his half-empty bottle of Shiner Bock, drained it, and ran back to the creek. As soon as I caught my breath, I rejoined Delbert and Gary in the water, and this time our fooling around involved more groping than roughhousing. Before long our peckers had become fence posts again.

I caught Gary from behind when he was thigh deep in the water, bent over to look at something, and I shoved my erect pecker between his ass cheeks.

He pulled away. 'Jesus, Carl, lube!'

'I'll bet it's cooled off by now.'

He glanced back at me and then ran toward shore. I took off after him and passed him when we reached dry land. I reached the cooler first and fished out the tube of lube. It hadn't just cooled down; it was cold. I experienced a little involuntarily shrinkage when I first applied it to my pecker.

Gary had reached me by then and I spun him around, bent him over the tailgate, slathered some lube into his ass crack, and again slipped my pecker between his cheeks. He was tight, but I grabbed his hips and pressed forward. His resistance lasted only a moment and then my pecker head slid deep inside him.

I drew back and plunged forward, then did it again. Because I was concentrating on boning Gary and wasn't paying any attention to what Delbert was doing, I didn't see him rise up from the creek and approach us from behind. I was surprised when I drew back and felt Delbert grab my hips and shove his pecker between my ass checks. He'd obviously lubed it up because it was slicker than snot, and when I shoved forward, he shoved forward, burying his pecker in my ass at the same time I buried mine in Gary's.

I've never been sandwiched before and it was unlike anything I'd even felt. We quickly found a rhythm, with me doing most of the work. As I drove into Gary, I pulled away from Delbert, and when I pulled back from Gary I impaled myself on Delbert.

Gary had one hand braced on the tailgate and used his free hand to stroke his pecker, beating like he was trying to whip up a meringue. He came first, spraying come across the ground beneath the Silverado, and I came a moment later, emptying myself inside Gary with a grunt. I collapsed against him, pinning him to the tailgate.

Delbert wasn't so easily satisfied. He took a half step forward as I leant against Gary and continued drilling into me, pounding harder and faster until he slammed into me one last time and erupted within me.

Then his weight as he collapsed against my back kept Gary and me trapped until Gary complained. 'Hey, guys, you're crushing me.'

Delbert finally pulled away, and then I followed.

I fished three Shiner Bocks from the cooler and passed them around. Then we stood in a rough circle, our peckers dripping come and lube, and drank until we'd slaked our thirst.

None of us felt like swimming after that so we cleaned up, pulled on our clothes, and headed back to town. Delbert dropped Gary off at his apartment and then dropped me off at my house.

Although I didn't realise it until that evening, I was sunburned in places that don't usually see sun, and it was several weeks before any of us could stand a slap on the back or a slap on the ass without wincing.

I know because we kept slapping each other just to see who would complain the loudest.

## A Trip to the Dark Side
## by Scarlet Blackwell

Some way through the evening, when they were both more than halfway drunk, Brian leant over and slurred in Will's ear. 'I want to introduce you to my favourite whore tonight.'

Will sighed and rolled his eyes because Brian always had a new favourite whore and Will really didn't need to pay for it.

'My treat,' Brian said with a grin and then put a finger on Will's lips before he could protest. 'Oh, wait till you see.'

Later, Will was too drunk to protest and kind of at the horny stage where he was confident he could still perform. Any more booze and it would be a waste, so he went along for the ride, so to speak. After all, he didn't have to do anything. He could just wank off and watch, couldn't he? He'd done threeways with Brian before and always been explicit beforehand – *we touch the girl, not each other*. Brian had always shrugged and said "whatever", and Will thought that implied Brian was easy and could go either way. Which wouldn't surprise him. Brian was about the most depraved man he'd ever met and would probably do a vacuum cleaner if no other hole was handy.

The brothel was somewhere in Covent Garden, somewhere round the back of a restaurant. Will didn't exactly look too closely; he just stumbled out of a taxi and followed Brian. He felt more sober when the cold night air hit him. More like picking up a takeaway and going on home.

Brian gripped him by the arm. 'Come on. Don't miss out on the best experience of your life.'

'OK, I'll have a little look and if she's not the hottest thing I've ever seen, I'm going home to bed and leaving you to it.'

Brian cackled. 'More for me,' he said as he knocked on a shuttered door and waited.

A small slot slid aside and a suspicious face peered at them before it relaxed. 'Hey, Brian, you just can't stay away, can you?'

Brian grinned ruefully as the door creaked open and stepped in, with Will following. They made their way down a gloomy corridor that opened into a vast, surprisingly cosy sitting room. Done up in red and gold, *naturellement*, with low level lighting, the place boasted couches and chairs on which reclined men in suits with half-dressed girls on their knees.

Will's cock stirred with interest. A tall brunette came over to them, eyeing him with a smile. 'Brian, darling!' She air-kissed Will's friend with scarlet lips. 'The usual?'

'Of course the usual,' Brian said. 'Is it all right if my friend watches?'

'I'm sure it is, but I'll just check.' She walked away, tapping buttons on a BlackBerry and speaking low into it, glancing over at Brian and Will.

Will looked around while they waited. Brian grabbed two champagne flutes off a tray carried by a waitress in a bunny tail and handed one to Will. Will shook his head. 'If you want me to be able to get it up, I'd better not have another.'

Brian shrugged because he never had that problem, no matter how much he drank, and set about the two glasses with gusto.

Their hostess returned. 'All right, gentlemen, go on up. You know the way.' She winked at Brian and took his glasses; as Will followed, she laid a delicate hand on his backside. 'You'll have a wonderful time.'

This whore, whoever she might be, was really being set up as something special. As someone who was generally bored with everything around him, tired of fucking the same plastic blonde every Friday night, tired of waking up regretting it, Will hoped he wasn't in for a massive disappointment. He followed Brian up a flight of red-lit stairs where his friend knocked on a door at the end of a long, winding corridor.

'Come in,' called a voice.

Brian grinned at Will and pushed the door open.

The room was small and neat, a king-sized bed dominating it, bedside tables carrying delicate, beaded lamps that cast a warm, peachy glow. Will closed the door after him. They waited as the sounds of running water stopped and a lean figure in a white dressing gown stepped from the bathroom.

Will stared. The woman had an exquisite face, elfin features framed by closely cropped blonde hair. Her dark blue eyes were made up in smoky colours, her lips painted red.

'You're not ready,' Brian said disapprovingly, as though this woman wasn't already an image. It made no difference to Will that she wore a bath robe rather than something sexy and he couldn't believe Brian was bothered either.

The woman pouted. 'I've just arrived,' she said in a husky voice. 'Don't be cross.'

'I'm not cross,' said Brian. 'I just like to see you in your clothes – and undress you.'

She smiled and stepped forward. 'You can undress me now.' Her gaze flickered to Will with interest. 'Who's your friend?'

'Will, this is Alex. Alex, Will. I wanted to show him *la crème de la crème* of London this evening.'

'You're very kind,' she demurred. She held out a small, delicate hand, the nails short and painted turquoise. Will took it. As she squeezed his palm, it sent a jolt to his cock. Oh God, she was – sensational.

'Do you want to play, Will?' she asked.

'I – don't know,' he stammered. Who was he trying to kid? His cock wanted to play all right and she knew it. She eyed the bulge in his pants and gave a soft laugh. Then she caught Brian by the wrist. 'Come here, big boy, I missed you.'

Brian embraced her, thick arms around a tiny waist, their mouths meeting in a needy kiss. Will stood and stared. He watched tongues dance and saliva swapped and he grew beyond hard, his cock throbbing.

He looked at the woman's body in the bathrobe. She had no spare fat, her curves neat and sparse, her chest somewhat flat, to his disappointment. Never mind, any more than a handful was a waste. Her legs were long and slender, her bare feet small and pretty. He stepped back to sit in a chair as Brian's whore started on his clothes, discarding his jacket and pulling his shirt open, and God, Will wanted a turn.

Brian shrugged his shirt off and unfastened his pants. He pushed Alex down on the bed. 'OK, let Will see what you've got,' he told her.

Alex unfastened the belt on her robe. She let it drop from her shoulders and tossed it away. Then she lay back on the bed with limbs splayed, beautiful body carefully posed and waited.

Will's greedy eyes slid down her body and his jaw dropped open. She was a *he*.

Alex had a flat, sculpted chest with two tiny pink nipples. A slight hint of dark hair arrowed down his belly to disappear behind the waistline of a pair of tighter than tight white briefs which were packed full to overflowing. Alex might have worn make-up, had delicate features and been undeniably androgynous, but he was all man.

Will gulped. He got up, glaring at Brian. 'This isn't funny.'

'Who's joking?' Brian said, kicking his shoes away and peeling off his socks. 'Isn't he the most beautiful thing you've ever seen? And such a slut too. He'll do anything you want, Will, and I mean anything.'

Will's gaze strayed back to the blond angel on the bed. He couldn't help but look again at the outline of thick, hard cock and heavy balls held prisoner behind the white fabric. He was disturbed to find his own hard-on hadn't waned one bit at this discovery.

Alex smiled coyly. He spread his legs some more and brushed the front of the briefs with the palm of one hand, cupping himself. 'Your friend is so fucking hot, Brian,' he purred, licking his lips. 'I want him inside me.'

Will's eyes must have bulged from his head. He turned and tried to leave before things got very complicated but Brian grabbed him by the wrist. 'Where are you going?'

Will tried to push him back. 'I'm not fucking queer, Brian,' he hissed under his breath. 'I didn't come here to fuck a bloke.'

'Listen to me,' Brian said. 'What's the difference? A hole's a hole and, believe me, he has the tightest hole you'll ever be in.'

Will caught his breath. His gaze strayed once more to the bed and he caught a glimpse of dark bush as Alex pushed a hand down his underwear with a smile. *Oh fuck.* Something bad was going to happen here. Something that meant Will would never be the same again. He stumbled back and sank once more into the chair. 'I'll just sit here,' he mumbled.

Brian smirked and patted him on the head. 'Sure you will.' He turned back to Alex. 'Now, where were we?' He pushed his pants and boxers down and climbed onto the bed with hard cock swaying between his legs.

Will tried not to squirm in his chair even as the sight of his friend naked conspired to turn him on. God, what was wrong with him? Was this what he secretly desired? He watched Brian and Alex entwine their bodies, passionately kissing, and his loins ached.

Brian pulled Alex on top of him. Alex kissed his way down Brian's body before settling between his legs, hand around Brian's hard shaft. He dipped his head and Will shifted in frustration because he couldn't see. He got up, walking around the side of the bed, and there he stared, watching Alex's painted mouth leave a red ring around the base of Brian's cock as he swallowed it whole.

'Fuck,' Will muttered. He stood watching Alex pull free, leaving Brian's erection glistening with saliva, then go down on him again, bobbing swiftly, his wet mouth wide. Will's breathing became unsteady. His gaze moved down the perfect curve of Alex's spine to his plump buttocks. Alex slid his eyes sideways. He knew Will was looking. He splayed his legs wide, feet hanging over the edge of the bed.

Will moved back to the chair at the end of the bed for a better view. Alex's bulge was neatly framed between his wide-spread legs, his arse cheeks straining against the thin, white material. As Will watched, the rent boy humped the bed, grinding himself, backside undulating.

Will chewed his lip and dug his nails into his palms. From the top of the bed, Brian grinned. 'Want to see what he's offering?' He gripped Alex under the arms and pulled him up his body. Alex lay there while Brian grabbed his buttocks, squeezing, massaging, before he slipped both hands down the white briefs, revealing arse crack and creamy flesh.

'Do you want to see or don't you?' Brian teased.

'Yes,' grunted Will helplessly.

Brian pushed the briefs down. A pair of shaven balls and a large dangling cock fell free. Alex helped him. He pulled his underwear down and off his legs, then he glanced back over his shoulder at Will with a grin and tossed the briefs his way.

Will caught them in one fist. He felt their warmth and he lowered them to his lap, his cock twitching.

Alex smiled at him. He slid back down Brian's body and went back to sucking him off, splaying his legs again. Will stared at the goods on offer. Between Alex's buttocks nestled the tiniest little hairless hole, pink and puckered and inviting.

Will ground his teeth and squeezed the underwear in his hand. Alex rose onto all fours and shook his arse at Will. He reached down and pushed his hard cock between his legs, poking it backwards at Will, where he lovingly massaged the drooling head.

Will lifted the briefs and spread them out between his hands. He saw the wet patch on the front and it made his blood surge with excitement. With the arousing sounds of Alex's slurping mouth ringing in his head, he lifted the material to his face and sniffed. He smelled Alex's musky, masculine smell, back and front. He put his tongue out and licked lightly at the wet patch.

'You dirty boy!' Brian laughed.

Alex lifted his head and looked over his shoulder. 'Come and be dirty with me,' he told Will.

Will shoved the underwear into his jacket pocket. Then he stood and started to strip.

Brian watched him, pushing Alex's mouth back to his task. 'Alex usually gets dragged up, padded bra and all. He's fooled a score of men and all of them have ended up fucking him. He's taken more men to the dark side than you've had hot dinners, Will.'

Alex mumbled something. He slid down further to mouth Brian's balls. Will dropped his boxers. Then he climbed onto the bed between Alex's spread legs.

With a trembling hand, he smoothed his palm over Alex's left buttock. Alex shivered and arched under his touch. Will touched his other cheek. Alex's creamy skin was satin soft. Will's fingers slid into the crack. Alex rose to his knees, arse presented wantonly, swaying under Will's touch.

Will lowered his face. Gently, he pressed a line of kisses over one cheek, trailing his hand over the other.

Alex gave a little groan. Will kissed him up to his lower back, encircling his torso with both arms, pressing his desperate hard-on against Alex's backside.

Alex whimpered. He knelt up, half-twisted his body around, hooked an arm around Will's neck and brought their mouths together.

Will thought he had died and gone to heaven. Oh God, Alex's mouth was so warm and soft and so fucking – tempting. There was no hope left for him. He held Alex closer, grinding his cock against his arse, sliding the head down Alex's cleft, precome lubricating his way.

Brian groaned. He sat up and started to enthusiastically

lick at Alex's rosy cockhead. Will looked over Alex's shoulder and watched Brian swallow the rent boy's cock. He couldn't get the last couple of inches in, on account of Alex being so big, but he had a damn good try.

Alex bucked forward, moaning. He reached back and gripped Will's backside, urging him closer, rocking back against his cock.

'Please,' he groaned. 'I need you to fuck me.'

Will's blood boiled. He pushed Alex forward and Alex toppled onto Brian and immediately moved into his groin again, sucking him off, backside lifted wantonly in the air. Will slid down off the edge of the bed to his knees. He gripped Alex's arse cheeks and pulled them apart while he had a little look at what he was about to get acquainted with.

Will was no stranger to back door love. But the only holes he knew were the fragrant rosebuds of women, not the sweaty holes of men. Still, the little pucker looked more inviting than he could ever believe. He dipped his head and ran his tongue down Alex's cleft, stopping shyly just short of the prize.

Alex jerked as though electrocuted. He started to pant and gasp. 'Oh God, yes!'

Brian cackled. 'You've found his Achilles' heel, Will. Alex likes a tongue in his arse to open him up, don't you, you filthy slut?'

He sat up, manoeuvring himself out from under Alex and slapped the rent boy on the arse hard.

Will jerked back as Alex flinched and groaned. He glanced unsurely at Brian, who knelt by Alex's head. 'He likes that,' Brian reassured him. 'Don't you?'

'Yes, yes,' Alex groaned with his head dipped and his arse presented for more. 'Please.'

Brian spanked him on the other cheek so it had a

matching red handprint and Alex jolted and shook.

Will stroked his own cock. He looked at Alex's flaming arse and then he spread it open again and flicked his tongue over the tight little hole.

Alex quivered and shouted in pleasure. Will set about him with brisk, wet strokes, working him slowly open, while Brian spanked his arse with hard slaps.

'Please … Please …' Alex cried.

'Don't you dare touch yourself,' Brian ordered, pushing Alex's hand from between his legs and slapping him again.

'No, sir,' Alex said, shaking with excitement with every lick to his soft, wet flesh.

'You come when we say you can come,' Brian told the rent boy.

'Yes, sir,' Alex said.

Will could barely control himself. The hole twitching and pulsing under his tongue, the flaming pink buttocks in his face, and the smell of arousal together with Alex's cries and moans of desperation. He pulled back and sat there panting, holding his cock.

'Fuck him,' Brian told him urgently. 'Fuck this little slut until he can't remember his own name.'

Alex let out another groan. He crawled up the bed and buried his face in the pillow with his arse thrust up and his ankles apart. He was wet, saliva tracking down his inner thighs and glistening on his balls. He reached for a tube of something from the bedside table and squirted some on his fingers. Will hurriedly rolled on the rubber Brian handed him, while he watched as Alex sought between his legs and fingered himself delicately, massaging lube into his already soaking entrance.

'Dirty boy.' Brian slapped one flaming cheek and Alex yelled.

Will pulled Alex's hand away. He lined himself up, gripping the base of his shaft and rubbed his cockhead against yielding wetness.

'Fuck, fuck …,' Alex wailed, trembling. 'Please, Will, please, I need you …'

Will pushed inside. He listened to Alex cry out and he didn't stop until he had given the rent boy every single glorious inch.

'Oh God, oh God.' Alex gasped and groaned. He bucked back, fucking himself on Will's cock.

Will growled. He grasped Alex's hips, withdrew and thrust back in. Brian watched with huge, lustful eyes, kneeling by their sides and wanking his own cock. 'Give it to him,' he said.

Will hardly needed the encouragement. He looked down, watching his dick disappearing into Alex's body, watching how his lover's spine undulated under Will's ministrations.

Fuck, *oh fuck*, Will was going to lose his mind.

He groaned loudly, lowered his head and pressed ardent kisses to Alex's sweat-dewed back.

'Give him a reach around,' Brian urged. 'You need to feel him come around your cock. It's the most amazing feeling in the world.'

Will did as he was told. He enclosed hard, solid flesh, the first prick he had ever touched apart from his own, and he slid his fist up and down, using his thumb to smear the precome around the head.

Alex nearly shouted. He pumped his cock into Will's hand and then pressed back onto his erection. He gasped and whimpered and panted, his body a delicious, writhing, sensual thing that took Will's breath away.

'That's it, that's it,' Brian panted. 'Come on, you slut, let me see you come.' He reached between their bodies, cupped both sets of balls, rubbing their two sacs together in a way which drove them both into a frenzy.

Alex started to yell. 'Yes! Yes! Oh God, Will, I'm coming, I'm coming!'

The bed rocked and squeaked, the headboard banging against the wall. Will fucked Alex harder, faster, deeper, feeling the rent boy's muscles convulsing around him, squeezing him into helpless climax.

Alex shuddered, limbs trembling uncontrollably. He spurted over Will's fingers in a torrent and Brian joined him with a shout, some of his spunk lacing both their hips. Will's friend immediately dropped down under Alex, where he started to eagerly suck the last drops from his cock.

The climax hit Will like a tsunami and swept him beneath wave upon wave of ecstasy. He cried out loud, continuing to jerk his hips forward steadily until Alex had milked him dry, and then he collapsed like a ton weight onto his lover's back.

Alex laughing softly beneath him, roused him from a stupor. 'You're crushing me.'

Will grunted and eased himself free, catching his condom as it slid off. He crawled to the foot of the bed, sitting there to tie a knot in it, blinking and trying to regain his scattered senses. Never had he felt so satiated, so – complete.

'Another notch on your bedpost for converting straight blokes, Alex,' Brian said. 'You can have double tonight.' He threw some notes on the bedside table.

An arm slid around Will's neck and hot skin pressed against his back. 'I would have done you for free,' Alex said into his ear.

Will shivered. His cock, unbelievably, started to stir. Even after everything, he wanted more. He put a hand up, to touch Alex's fingers.

'Give me your phone number,' he said in a whisper.

Alex's soft lips sucked at the lobe of his ear before he moved to kiss the nape of Will's neck. 'Are you sure?'

'I'm sure,' Will said.

'Don't mind me,' Brian said, climbing off the bed and disappearing into the bathroom.

Alex moved away. He got up and Will watched his slender figure as he located his bath robe on the floor and pulled it on. His eyeliner was smudged, smeared lipstick around his mouth, and his cheeks were flushed. He looked like he'd just been thoroughly and utterly fucked.

Will smiled.

Alex returned it, his teeth perfect and pearly, his topaz eyes glittering mischievously. Will reached out, gripped Alex's wrist and guided him onto his lap. As they kissed, he put his hands below Alex's robe, smoothing over his bare backside, a finger seeking his still-wet heat and sheathing itself inside.

Alex squirmed with a gasp. He clutched Will's face, looking down into it. 'Stay here with me tonight.'

Will squinted towards the thin curtains covering the window. 'It's nearly dawn now.'

'Then stay until you've fucked me into a coma.'

Will grinned. His hand closed around Alex's stiffening cock. Their lips met again, Alex's tongue playing with his.

The bathroom door opened and Brian started to noisily dress. 'Are we going or what?'

'I'm staying here a while.'

Brian narrowed his eyes. He stared at Will and then addressed Alex. 'You're fucking unbelievable,' he told the rent boy.

Alex smirked. 'I know.' He rocked on the finger in his

arse. 'What can I say? I like corrupting straight boys.'

Will knew he should have been offended. He knew he should have been leaving and putting the experience down to a big, alcohol-fuelled mistake. When he woke up later today, he would find used underwear in his pocket and surely regret this night for ever. But he didn't care about any of that. His dick was rigid and ready to go again.

'I want you to ride my hard cock until you come all over me, you little slut,' he told Alex.

Alex squirmed in excitement. 'Yes sir.'

Brian paused in dressing. 'OK,' he said. 'I'm just going to sit over here and watch quietly.'

Alex grinned. He tossed off his robe and climbed from Will's lap to retrieve a rubber off the bedside table.

Will watched him all the way with his blood singing in his veins, feeling, for the first time in a long while, truly alive.

Alex turned back and caught the expression on his face. He straddled Will's hips, rolled on the condom and rubbed his backside teasingly against Will's throbbing cock.

'Do you want it?' he asked.

'I want it,' said Will. He closed his eyes and took Alex's lips with his own as Alex sank right down on his cock and Will floated away into bliss.

## Bless Me Father
## by Heidi Champa

'Bless me Father, for I have sinned.'

I almost laughed as I said it. But I tried to be serious. The whole illusion wasn't going to work unless I could play the part. I cleared my throat and tried to stifle the giggles that kept bubbling up, but it wasn't working. It was all just too surreal.

'It's been for ever since my last confession.'

My voice broke on the last word and I doubled over. I couldn't see him, but his words told me he was less than thrilled.

'Stop it, this isn't funny any more.'

He was uncomfortable, I could tell. He was also intrigued, but he would never admit it. At least not yet. I broke character for a moment and tried to get him back on board.

'Come on. Loosen up, where's your sense of humour?'

I pushed him, wanting to have a little fun.

'Someone might find us in here.'

Our little confession rooms were right there at the back of the church. He was right; anyone could have come in and found us. That was part of the fun. Wasn't it?

'So? What are they going to do? Arrest us for sitting in a confessional?'

'No. It's just – it's not something to mess around with, that's all.'

Spoken like a true altar boy. God bless him, he was still so good. Almost too good. I would be lying if I didn't say that part of what turned me on about him was how deeply good he was. And, the fact that I got to be the dirty one.

'Oh right. If we do we might go to hell.' I smiled again in the dark, shifting on my little seat. It creaked as I moved, and I feared that it would snap and break if I kept it up.

The air in the confessional was musty and dry. I could just make out his face through the fancy lattice work between us. I was new to this whole experience, while he spent four years in this place, a traditional seminary prep boarding school, thinking he wanted to be a priest. It didn't work out that way, obviously. He probably spent a lot of time in this tiny space, telling the priest all about his swearing, impure thoughts, and the like. Now we were back, a long overdue trip down memory lane. But I couldn't help it if I felt naughty. Not that it was an unusual feeling for me.

There was something in me, always compelling me to do the wrong thing. My desperate urge to say "bomb" on an airplane. My theft of my neighbour's newspapers, just to throw them away. Telling him I wasn't wearing underwear in church that morning. Things like that. That last fact made him squirm in his seat, his jaw set tightly. Despite his surroundings, I had made him think about my bare cock underneath my pants. I knew he was both angry and turned on by my secret. Just hearing the words would make him think about the two of us, back at our hotel, his hot lips wrapped around my cock, sucking me until I begged him to fuck my ass. All that going on in his head while he tried to pay attention to the priest at the front of the church. I knew it was the exact wrong thing to do, but

I couldn't help it. I had a hard-on most of the service, which had to be some kind of terrible sin, right?

What would the Lord think? I mean, He could see me, right? He could tell what I was doing. Or so I've been told.

We managed to get through the service, and now that the place had cleared out, we could have a lot more fun. I could hear him moving next to me in his booth, trying to get comfortable on his own creaky wooden seat. They were obviously a matched set. I let my legs fall open, my cock again straining against the fabric of my pants. I was starting to feel a bit raw, with no boxers between me and my summer suit trousers. I was hot and so blasphemously hard under that fabric. I had gone with a conservative look for the occasion, but somehow managed to forget to slip on the black boxers I'd packed specifically for the day. Thou shalt wear underwear wasn't a commandment, was it?

'Anyway, like I said, I have sinned.'

He didn't respond, so I went on.

'I've been having some very bad thoughts. About my boyfriend. You see, father, I want to have sex with him. Even though I'm not supposed to have sex with another guy. It's wrong, isn't it? I mean, I've heard that the Catholic Church frowns on homosexuality. So fucking my boyfriend would be very, very wrong. Right? I mean, even though we're basically married. I mean, not that we can even get married, but you see my point, right?'

He hesitated before playing along with me, probably just to get me to stop.

'Yes, it is. Very wrong. There, are you happy? Can we please get out of here now?'

He was trying to stay composed, to stay away from my temptation, but I knew I was getting through. I could just

177

hear the strain in his voice, the desire seeping through the mature façade he had kept up all morning. I knew if I kept going, I might just get him to go over to the dark side, to put his goodness aside, just for a few minutes. Even though I knew it was so very wrong, it clicked something in my head and I just couldn't resist the sweet pleasure of something so devilishly naughty.

'Also, in addition to the sex, every night, before I go to sleep, I have impure thoughts. Really impure thoughts.'

I waited for his reply, knowing that he was still trying to decide what to do. Should he play along with me, or should he shut down my little game? After a few moments of hesitation, I got my answer.

'What kind of thoughts?'

He was getting into it, despite himself. I slid my hand to my zipper and pulled it down. I let my cock spring free before wrapping my fist around it, giving it a slight tug. Through the screen, I heard the faint sound of his breath, his palms rubbing across the fabric of his suit pants.

'Naughty thoughts. Things I want to do to him, and that I want him to do to me.' I smiled as touched myself, knowing that it was wrong. Very wrong. I looked to the little screen and saw him trying to look at me through it, to see what I was up to. But I think he already knew. I slid my hand up and down my cock slowly, waiting on his next words.

'Can you be more specific?'

He was breathing heavy now, trying to stay calm, stay in his role of the caring priest.

'Well, there is one thing that I think about the most.'

'What's that?'

His voice was filled with expectation, waiting for my dirty thoughts. I could almost taste the anticipation. I made him wait a few painful seconds before I answered him. My cock was aching for release, but the sweet torture of the tease was so amazing, I could have stayed that way all day.

'I think about sucking his cock, really deep into my throat. Over and over and over again. And letting him come in my mouth. I want to feel him come down the back of my throat.'

There was silence on the other side of the wall. I stopped jerking myself off and held my breath for a moment before I continued, trying to find the strength to hold myself back. I didn't want to push him too hard.

'But is oral sex still wrong? Or is it only fucking each other in the ass that is the problem?'

I let my fingers creep up over the head of my cock, the tip full and swelled with blood. I could feel my moisture, my precome starting to drip. I was a little surprised how turned on this whole thing had made me. Every little thing about it was playing havoc with my senses. I was desperate to come, but I curled my toes and held off. I felt my balls tighten slightly, my body tense and sweaty. His voice cut through my private thoughts.

'Well, I'm sure you know that oral sex and sex are the same in the eyes of God.'

'But there's more, Father. Much more. After I suck him off, I let him play with my ass, put his fingers inside me. I let him put his tongue on it, and lick me until I feel like I'll go crazy.'

I couldn't resist moving my fist up and down my cock again. I also couldn't stop the groans that were now coming out of my mouth. The sound filled the quiet of the tiny room, and I was sure he could hear me. I wondered if he was as excited as I was, if his cock was straining against those navy blue wool pants he'd chosen especially for the day. It was his favourite suit. I put my other hand on my balls and toyed with them as I got closer to the proverbial edge.

'We have to stop this, someone might come back.'

I heard the panic in his protests. I thought he had gotten into our little game. But the good part of him was still trying to break through. Bless his little heart.

'If you're not going to stay in character, this isn't going to work. Just relax and enjoy it. You know you want to. And I know that I do. I'm so fucking close to coming all over the place in here.'

I could hear him open his mouth to protest again, but it never came out. He didn't say another word. Part of him was still that obedient boy who spent his youth at this church, in this box. Part of him would always relish the traditions, even if he didn't practice the church's tenets any more. I could smell sex, filling the tiny little room. I wondered if he could smell it too. My cock swelled even more as I kept jerking myself off, building the pressure and tension until I thought I was going to explode. Teasing myself, I heard him clear his throat in the next compartment. He was ready to get back into his role.

'So you've already had sex with this boyfriend of yours?'

I could hear the laugh behind his voice; he was trying to stay serious.

'Remember, you have to tell me the truth, or confession is meaningless. Tell me the truth.'

'Well, Father, the real truth is we have sex. A lot. I let him fuck me on the second date. He fucks my ass so good. So I guess there really isn't any point in me trying to be good now. Is there?'

I slid my fist over my cock again, my orgasm so very close. My breathing was ragged and loud, my whole body begging for release.

'I think you will always have a problem with being a bad boy. There may be little hope of reforming you. But I think we should still try to make you good.'

He sounded so wonderfully naughty, so very bad. I wiped my thumb over the drop of precome that was clinging to my skin. As the pad of my thumb slipped and slid, I was about to ask for my penance when we both heard footsteps coming towards us. He exited first, confronting the priest who had taught him so many years ago. I straightened myself out, zipped up my pants, and came out from behind the curtain with my suit jacket in front of my still bulging cock, just as he was explaining how I'd always wanted to see the inside of a confessional. The priest gave us a smile, and admonished us for goofing off with a sacrament of the Holy Catholic Church. I nodded solemnly and he apologised profusely. We shook hands, and I took no small joy in knowing what very nearly took place in that confessional, how close I was to coming all over that tiny space. My little altar boy dragged me out to the car, so we could make our way to the hotel.

'I told you we'd get caught. God, that was embarrassing. At least he didn't see your hard-on.'

He started the car angrily.

'I never got to ask what my penance is for having such dirty thoughts.'

He shot me a nasty look, before his lips curled into a smile. I knew I had him back, and I smiled back at his gorgeous face.

'Oh well. I think I can remember what the punishment is for behaviour like that.' We drove down the tree-lined street and his hand settled between my legs, my cock responding to his firm touch. I was so glad he hadn't become a priest. It would have been such a tragic waste.

# Lock, Cock and Two Smoking Arseholes
## by Marcus Swannick

I'll tell you now, for the proverbial record, I've never officially been a member of the Double Deuces gang. Far from it.

For one, I've never been keen on their mob-handed bravado, no matter what they get up to. I prefer to think of myself as a professional businessman – a successful wheeler and dealer, with an interest in any deal which makes me money. In the pecking order around here, I consider myself to be the guy who would call them in when *I* want a job doing.

The other thing is their leader, Ky. Don't get me wrong here, he's a real diamond who I've known for some time. He's someone I used to go to school with and even before we'd left the Secondary Modern we had a friendship that was solid. I would be the brains behind various business ventures while he had the connections. Not always successful, I'll give you that, but we still managed to turn a quid or two.

Our personal friendship and business partnership has lasted beyond our teens and into our 20s – even when Ky went on to join the gang as a runner, then finally became the leader of the Double Deuces. I decided there was more profit to be had from playing it solo, which is why I've moved on from running some lines and long firms to owning some very nice and accommodating lock-ups I found going begging in several of the backstreets around and about.

Also, of course, there's no way I'm prepared to get a fucking tattoo of two playing cards on my arm. I've got enough bottle and can do the business whenever I want, but you can shove the idea of some wanker coming at me with an electric fucking needle!

Anyway, some deals hadn't gone as smooth as they could have and I needed Ky's help to shift some moody gear that one of my own crew had picked up by mistake. That was why I was hanging around the Prince William pub on Shenley Street late on Friday evening. As usual, I had found a spot at the front bar and had already been waiting several minutes for one of Ky's crew to at least ask me what the fuck it was I wanted.

Finally, Dizzy – a campy queen who was regularly to be found under the tables at Christmas, dishing out the blowjobs – spotted me from behind the bar, and after a respectful "Oh lawd, luv! Is that gear back in fashion again?" he finally minced off to let Ky know I wanted to see him. You can say what you will about Dizzy, but when things start kicking off and turning nasty I'm more than happy to have him covering my back.

One of the barmaids got me a bottle of Export Extra from behind the bar and I'd almost finished it when Dizzy came back. 'You're out of luck at the moment, sweetheart. His lordship's still going to be some time with another deal.' He grinned at me and added, 'If you need something to pass the time …'

I finished off the Extra, waved the bottle at him, and then belched. He looked at me in mock horror. 'Lawd! That stuff'll turn you butch, I swear it will!' he chirped, before going off to get me another from the chiller.

A couple of bottles later and Ky finally comes out

through the front bar, seeing a pair of upmarket nightclub owners to the door, before turning around and greeting me with a broad smile.

'Billy! Always a pleasure, mate.'

I smiled back and told him I needed to discuss some business and could we go to his office rather than talking about it at the bar? With a look and a nod to Dizzy, both of us went through the back and up the stairs to his second-floor office cum crib – a neat little one-bedroom flat far enough above the pub so as to be quiet even when downstairs got a bit rowdy.

Despite our friendship it still took a while for us to be up front with each other, and we had just finished working out a deal which suited the pair of us when Dizzy knocked on the door. He handed Ky a large set of keys. 'That's everything sorted and everyone kicked out for the night, love. I'm off up the Heath to find a handjob and then home.'

Ky tossed the keys onto a side table. 'Don't forget the brewery will be dropping off some of those guest beers early tomorrow morning, so if you want to get a gobful of Nick Pirelli's salami then you'd better not be late.'

'Never missed a delivery yet, ducks!' And with that he was off down the stairs and out through the side door.

Thankfully I had nothing to rush back to my crib for, and when Ky asked me if I fancied a drink before heading back, I thought I might as well. Trouble is I had started to get up, saying I'd just have a quick JD on the rocks, but somewhere along the line I felt a little light-headed and ended up colliding into Ky as I tried to steady myself. Quick as a flash, he caught hold of my arm and managed to stop me from falling over the coffee table, a look of real concern on his face.

Holding on to him, I said I was OK. 'It's probably

down to all the stress of having the dodgy gear turning up out of the blue and having to hang on to it while it's still warm.' But for some reason I didn't let go of his arm. There was something about the situation which seemed to put me in a totally different place. I could smell his warmth and the whiff of his aftershave gave me an odd tingling sensation inside. I kept looking at his light brown hair, his green eyes, the line of his nose and his jaw … The next thing I know, I've moved in close, up front and personal, and kissed him firmly on the mouth!

I don't know what I had been originally expecting, but before I knew what the hell was happening Ky was pulling me into him, his mouth opening up and his tongue probing at my lips until I finally opened up to him and sucked his tongue into my mouth.

After a moment we stopped kissing and pulled apart. Looking at me, he just smiled. 'I wondered how long it would be till you finally came across. I knew, deep down, you didn't seem comfortable with all that girl stuff.'

He knew he was right. We'd been best mates for so long he knew I'd never really had a successful relationship with a woman. I was about to protest when he leant forward and kissed me deeply again.

'Kick your shoes off, Billy.'

I did, feeling the carpet beneath my toes and the electric tingle starting back up inside me. Without saying a word, he just took hold of my hand and slowly led me into the bedroom.

Turning the lighting down low, he slipped off my jacket and put it carefully to one side on a chair in the corner. Slowly he undid my tie and threw it on top of the jacket before his strong fingers carefully unbuttoned my shirt, pulling it free of my trousers before removing it completely. My breathing was already deep and heavy but when he pulled me up closer and I felt his hands start unbuckling my belt, I could feel myself starting to almost groan with pent-up excitement.

With one hand he ran his palm up over my stomach and chest, purposely cupping it around my pec, and with the other he slowly unzipped my fly and let my trousers fall around my ankles, revealing my white briefs and, straining behind them, my stiff cock. Sliding his hands over my body and into the small of my back, he deliberately pulled me in close and kissed me long and hard, and I could feel him smile as I inwardly moaned at the pleasure he was giving me.

Breaking away momentarily he slipped his hands under my armpits and literally lifted me clear of my trousers, and I closed my eyes for a second, unsure of where things were going to go next. But when I opened them I looked down and saw he was kneeling in front of me, then the surge of sensations as his hands slid up my thighs, hooking his thumbs into the white waistband and the feel of the material as he slowly peeled down my briefs, finally exposing my rock-hard prick.

'My, my, Billy, you have come on since those days in the gym.'

Carefully taking my stiff cock in one hand, he slowly moved his fist up and down, and when his other hand moved up to touch me under my balls the rush I felt was such that I was sure I would black out.

Looking up at me, he smiled knowingly. 'I think for your sake we should maybe slow things down a little.'

Standing up again, he gently moved me backward then, almost picking me up, he carefully got me on my back in the middle of the double bed. He moved down to the end and leant over me a little to remove my socks – leaving me stark bollock naked and with my hard cock stiff and proud – before he started to slowly strip in front of me.

Deliberately he undid his shirt and let it drop to the floor, revealing the scoop vest underneath, which flashed off his nicely defined biceps and forearms. Then, in one single movement, the vest was pulled up over his head and also just allowed to fall to the floor, revealing his smooth, trim stomach and chest. Looking at me with a warm, confident smile, he undid the waistband of his jeans and then slowly popped each fly stud open, one at a time, revealing his own stiff cock little by little. Ky always went commando style, whatever the occasion, and the effect of seeing his hard cock slowly being exposed was totally fascinating. He let the faded blue denim hang there for a moment until, with a shrug of his hips, his jeans fell away to reveal an impressively thick seven-inch cock and large balls to match – the swollen head pushing his foreskin back and already dribbling a little precome.

Still smiling at me, he said, 'Don't worry, Billy. Everything is going to be just fine.'

Stepping out of his jeans he moved onto the bed and immediately straddled my stomach, reaching out to purposefully take hold of my wrists before pinning them down above my head. Bending forward he kissed me and bit at my lip, before moving down to kiss and lick at my throat. I had never felt so helpless and yet so powerful before, and the combination of emotions was making me almost pant with excitement.

Pushing himself back upright again, he brought my still-held arms with him, shifting his grip to my hands before he deliberately placed them flat against his taut stomach. His skin felt hot and dry as he started to move them around in little circles – rippling his muscles at the same time – before slowly pushing my hands down lower, into his pubic hair and then onto his large cock.

Still holding my hands he wrapped one around his shaft, and the other he slipped up to cup his balls, and I suddenly realised he was stroking and playing with himself through me. I tried several times to speed up the pace, but every time I did he would deliberately hold my hands firm, slowing the movement down to a lazy back and forth again.

'No need to rush, Billy. We've got plenty of time to just let things happen. Anyway, I don't think you're quite ready for my length of meat inside you just yet. It's a little on the thick side, and I know you've not had your arse fucked before. Maybe later, when you've found out what pleasure really is, I'll let you take it.'

To be honest, I was just happy I was in the position of being given a chance to touch and fondle this guy I had known since our shared schooldays. I might not have been able to trust him totally in business, but here, on top of the bed, I felt he could do anything he wanted and I'd still be safe.

Reaching across me, he opened a bedside drawer and took out a sachet of what I knew was a water-based lubricant, and in the past I'd seen Dizzy handing out something similar to his friends before they'd disappeared off somewhere. Tearing off the end he squeezed the contents out into the palm of his hand and then reached around behind his back.

I'll never forget that first cold kiss of lubricant on my stiff cock or the way his fingers and palm changed from something dry and gripping to something slick, his middle finger sliding down to rub and tease at my balls for a moment. Then he was bending forward, his still-slick hand fingering his own arse and slipping some lubricant up himself. Before I really knew what was happening, Ky was deliberately edging himself backward a little, and I felt him firmly taking my slippery cock in his hand, and placing it right up against his arsehole.

Looking directly at me, he said, 'This is what it's all about, baby. This is all just for you.'

Then he started to slowly rock himself back and forth on top of me, and I could feel the head of my cock pushing against, then slowly slipping into Ky's arse, a little at a time, until, with a grunt, he rocked backward and I felt the head push its way past his ring and start sliding into him for real.

I just lay there and let him lead for a while, a look of serenity on his face as he gently pushed down, until my cock was buried up to my tight balls in his arse, making me realise just how much pleasure I was giving him. But the way he slowly rocked himself back and forth encouraged me, and I still remember the way he smiled when I impulsively took hold of his cock and started to wank him off in time to his movements.

With his hot arse gripping me and with him expertly riding me, it wasn't long before I was thrusting up with my hips and frantically working his cock, revelling in the way it jerked and twitched in my hand. I could smell the hot mustiness coming from his body as he worked on my cock, and the sexually heady smell of his precome as it oozed and dribbled over the back of my hand and knuckles, aware all the time of the way his large, hairy balls rubbed and bounced on my stomach.

Suddenly, I felt him move. Reaching a hand behind himself he lightly brushed his fingertips over my balls, then moved his hand down and around until, with a sudden push, he thrust a lube-coated finger firmly up my arse. And then I was coming – pushing up with my hips as he was pushing down, grinding his arse into my groin, forcing my cock even deeper, trying almost to suck my balls up into his wonderful arse. Moments later he was grunting and snorting like some angry bull, throwing his head and chest back and literally firing shot after explosive shot of come over me, splashing my hair and my cheek, and landing hotly on my lips and neck.

When we had finally both got our breaths back, Ky slowly rolled off and lay beside me on the bed. A little breathlessly he said, 'I'm going to grab a shower, check the alarms, and then catch up on some sleep.' He looked a little expectantly at me, his tongue running along the edge of his lower lip. 'I don't suppose you want to stay the night? Dizzy's actually very good at being discreet. Plus he makes a mean breakfast fry-up for the early staff. I mean –' he broke off for a moment, then '– there's always the couch in the lounge if you want?'

I just grinned and licked some of him off the back of my hand. 'What do you think?'

Of course, every favour has its payback. So when Ky asked me three weeks later to do a little bit of client minding, I wasn't really in any position to say no, now was I?

That was why I was back in the Prince William pub on what felt like one of the rowdier Friday nights of the month. The hectic situation wasn't being helped by Dizzy throwing a bit of a hissy fit. From the dagger-loaded looks he kept giving a couple of flamboyant Marys who would probably have been more at home down Old Compton Street than there in the bar, I suspected Dizzy was getting territorial in his old age.

Ordering a bottle of Becks I played devil's advocate. 'I didn't know you'd abdicated?'

Dizzy glared at me, and I knew immediately he was

hyped up for something confrontational. 'Listen up, pretty boy. There's only one ruling monarch in this pub, and this queen is still on the throne! Now, if you'll excuse me, I have some eyes to scratch out!'

Thankfully before anything tasty kicked off the pub door opened and in walked my returning favour in the form of Ahmed Jidakh. Ky had asked me to keep an eye out for the young Arab-looking guy, and when he turned up at the Prince I was supposed to play the part of mein host. I didn't have anything planned, mainly as I'd never met the guy before, and depending on how bad his long-haul flight had been he might not have been up for much anyway. It also looked like he had flown in without any luggage or overnight bag, so I decided to stick with my original intention of just taking him upstairs to Ky's flat. Once I'd shown him the facilities, I'd planned on just ordering a takeaway and letting him relax until his lordship turned up later on.

Ky was going into the glass-and-brass bling and knockoff business, intending to shift the moody merchandise through various East and North London street markets, probably over half a dozen weekends. Ahmed was his contact from Dubai. He had been over once before with a batch of fake Rolexes as part of a goodwill package and Ky had been allowed to check them out before deciding whether or not they were worth the effort.

Looking at him standing in the pub doorway I could easily see that under his sharp suit and tie he kept his body just as sharp and trim. He stood around 5 foot 9, slim build, short but not cropped black hair, and with that natural Arabic tan to his skin. But the thing which really caught my attention the most had been his smoulderingly dark and expressive eyes which seemed to be slowly

191

taking in everything and everyone with a single sweep of the bar.

I'm not sure if Ky had given him a rough description of what I looked like or not. But when his gaze met mine his lips curved slightly in a soft smile and he immediately came over and introduced himself. He had what I can only say was a confident walk, and an almost arrogant air to him, but when it came to the introductions his handshake was warm and friendly. It also seemed to linger a lot longer than I expected it to.

'Am I right in thinking you are Ky's friend, Billy?' He smiled, showing off perfect white teeth.

''Fraid so.' I pointed offhandedly over the bar. 'Can I get you a drink or something? Unless alcohol's against your religion, but I'm sure there's bottles of fruit juice or something back there you can drink instead.'

He leant towards me a little as if to make himself heard, and rested his hand on my chest. 'I'm fine with alcohol, but I'm going to have to decline your hospitality.' Under my shirt the palm of his hand felt warm against my chest and when he moved a little I felt my nipple starting to stiffen up as Ahmed continued, 'It's been a long and uneventful flight. If we could go somewhere less crowded? I just want to relax and ease away some of the stress for a while.'

Still very conscious of the effects of his hand, I said, 'No problem. Ky's told me to keep you entertained until he gets back, so whatever you want to do is fine by me.' I was never into the babysitting lark anyway, and if truth be known, I did have other things to see and other people to do. But favours are favours, and I couldn't see any point in creating bad blood between us, especially if Ky was going to be working with the guy.

I led the way through the back of the bar and up the

several flights of stairs to Ky's crib, and when Ahmed walked through the door he paused and nodded appreciatively. Dropping his jacket on one of the easy chairs he slowly pulled off his tie and kicked his shoes off, then he took a leisurely tour of the lounge. Ky has some nice stuff, and none of it cheap and tacky either, and it wasn't long before Ahmed stopped in front of a piece of sculpture Ky was pretty fond of. It's a raw plaster of Paris torso of a naked man, and I could see exactly where Ahmed's gaze was. Hardly surprising, as the artist had left *nothing* to the imagination! I always said anything that big just had to be a deformity. Hell, you'd need a fucking blood transfusion just to get it semi-hard!

Ahmed glanced inquisitively at me while he reached out and let his fingers play over the sculpture for a moment or two, and I remembered the heat of his hand on my chest. Then he moved, coming up close to me, and I felt his hand cup my cock and balls through my trousers – both of us feeling my cock swelling and pushing against the cotton of my boxer shorts. The next thing I knew he was kissing me hard on the lips, his tongue forcing its way between them and into my mouth. Without any hesitation I put a hand to the back of his head and pulled his mouth harder onto mine, deliberately taking control, and let my other hand ride down his back to fondle and squeeze his arse. Pushing my groin firmly against his, I was sure he was getting wise to the fact I really wanted to slide my cock into him.

Between us I could feel his fingers move downwards, then the zip of my trousers being pulled open, and his warm, dry, and eager fingers freeing my cock from my boxers, out into the open air.

Slowly he traced the outline of my cock with his fingertips, slipping the foreskin backward and forward a few times, the head getting slippery with precome, as he whispered, 'Ah! You are intact!'

In a brief flurry of movements he undid my waistband then pushed my trousers and boxers down around my ankles. Then he was down in front of me, engulfing my cock with his hot mouth, even taking a length of it down his throat so I could feel his nose and mouth pressing against my stomach and groin. Slowly he moved his head backward, letting his lips tighten around my shaft as my cock slipped out of his throat and into his mouth again. Then he went to work on it with his tongue – licking the shaft, running the tip of his tongue around and sometimes under the foreskin, flicking it in and out of my piss-slit, and generally driving me wild.

After a moment or two I pulled his head off my cock and helped him stand up, immediately getting my hands on his trousers. Two seconds later I was pushing them and his tight briefs down below his knees, exposing his stiff and golden circumcised cock in all its glory. I couldn't resist. I reached down and took hold of it.

His eyes closed and a smile of pleasure crossed his lips as I continued to stroke his cock with one hand, then slipped two fingers of the other into his mouth, feeling his tongue slide over them, his lips clamp down and start to move over them in time with the movements of my cock-stroking hand.

I've not had the chance to play with many circumcised cocks, but I must have been doing something right because in moments the palm of my hand was smeared with warm, sticky trails of precome.

Then Ahmed broke away, stepped out of the pile of clothes around his ankles, and after I had done the same, he led me to the large sofa. Eagerly I sat down and, in a flash, he was straddling my legs, lifting up the ends of his shirt, and presenting me with his rock-hard golden cock.

I didn't need any encouragement and sucked as much of it as I could into my mouth – the sticky taste of it was strong and tangy, and the feel of my tongue on his cockhead brought several uninhibited moans of pleasure from deep within him. For a moment I pulled away from him, drenched a couple of fingers in spit, and then sucked his cock back into my mouth – not wanting to miss any of this free action. Cupping his balls with one hand, I slid the other with the wet fingers between his legs, around his ball sack, and started to push and probe at his arsehole – feeling it relax and then tighten as I pushed first one, then two fingers into him, getting him lubricated up and ready for my throbbing cock.

As if on cue, he pulled away, turned himself around and moved toward me, presenting me with his firm, golden globes. Never one to look a gift arse in the mouth, I parted his cheeks and dove straight in with my tongue, jamming it into him as I had done with my fingers, until his arsehole was sopping wet. Then, placing my hands on his hips, I pulled him down hard and fast into my lap, spearing him on my cock in one downward thrust that was started by me, but more than joyfully finished by Ahmed himself, pushing down and twisting his hips – trying to get as much of my cock into him as possible.

In seconds we were bouncing up and down on the sofa – one part of me fucking him for all I was worth, and another praying and hoping that we'd both be satisfied before the springs gave out!

Not breaking the rhythm, Ahmed took one of my hands off his hip and, holding it by the wrist, brought it up to his mouth and started licking the palm and fingers. It was a weird sensation, I can tell you! The next thing I know, he spits into my palm twice before pushing my hand down into his groin and wrapping my fingers around his cock.

So there I was with my own cock buried deep into Ahmed's tight and hot arse while his beautiful cock was getting well and truly wanked off with my hand – albeit with a little help from Ahmed himself.

Within moments I could feel the tingling starting down in my balls and my cock becoming almost painfully rigid, both tell-tale signs I was about to shoot my load right up this glorious Arab's arse. Ahmed must have sensed something because he took my hand from his cock, shoved it between his legs so as to cup his tight ball sack, and started furiously to wank himself off as fast as he could while still bouncing up and down on my cock.

Then I was exploding inside him, pushing myself up and arching my back in one last almighty push before I felt spurt after spurt of hot come shooting from my cock. Ahmed's hand became a blur for a moment or two and then he threw his head back – nearly headbutting me in the process! – and I swear I could hear his come as it splashed across his shirt front in thick ropes of sticky white liquid.

Later, after we had showered and Ahmed had changed into some of Ky's spare gear, we sat around talking about his business propositions. When I finally left him gently blissing out and went back to my own crib, I was feeling really happy, knowing that although Ahmed might be selling fakes, I had at least been fucking the real thing.

## Looking Out for Trouble
### by Elizabeth Coldwell

I shouldn't even be working tonight. That wasn't the plan. By rights, I should be with Gaz and Paddy and Millsy, out of our heads on cheap Greek booze and looking to get my end away. Instead, I'm standing here, watching the rain pissing it down, shivering even in my thick Crombie and counting the minutes till the club shuts and I can go home.

Gaz came up with the idea, over a pint in the Duke. One of those last-minute holiday deals you can pick up on the Internet: a cheap flight out of Robin Hood Airport and a couple of nights in Zante or Paros or Santorini; one of those resorts that's glamorous and exciting in all the ways this place isn't. And, more importantly, somewhere summer's already arrived.

He never said it, but we all knew why he wanted to get away. Karen, bending his ear again, wanting to know when he's going to move out of his mum's place and in with her, taking their relationship to what she calls "the next level". The sort of talk that has him shuddering and coming out in a cold sweat at the thought. Commitment and Gaz aren't two words you'd ever hear in the same sentence, but she still doesn't seem to have figured it out yet. And when Karen gets too clingy, Gaz gets the urge to run.

Me, I was hoping for the chance to feel the sun on my back and maybe, just maybe, get off with a guy for a few hot, sweaty hours of passion. I'm not the sort who normally goes in for one-night stands and the thrills only a stranger can offer, but it's been months since I last had a decent fuck. Not since Tony and I … But this isn't the time to be thinking about Tony. I'm miserable enough as it is.

Though the lads will tell you I've always been unlucky in love. It's a more unexpected spot of bad luck that means I'm stuck here while they're having fun in the sun. As soon as I'd told Gaz I'd got the time off, I was in, and he could start looking for the best deal for the four of us, the head gasket blew on my Punto, leaving me looking at a hefty repair bill. There's no way I can manage without the car for any length of time, not when the club doesn't close till 3 a.m., and my funds are limited to say the least, so bye bye Santorini, hello Masbrough Auto Repairs.

At least the guy who fixed my gasket offered something in the way of consolation, with his thick, dark curls and eyes as blue as the Aegean. Wide, capable looking hands too, and all set off with this cute little smudge of engine grease on his cheek. While he was breaking the cost of repairing the damage, I couldn't stop my mind wandering to what he might look like with those oil-stained blue overalls of his half off, revealing a muscular body, honed by hard manual work, and a dark treasure trail down his chest, leading all the way to a thick, slowly uncurling cock.

If he caught me staring at him, more than likely with lust etched all over my face, he didn't say anything. But when I went back to collect the car yesterday morning, there was the briefest of moments when I thanked him for the job he'd done, grasped his hand – and sensed a definite connection. The smile in his eyes mirrored my own, acknowledging my desire and offering the glorious promise of fulfilment. Then the moment passed and we were just two men shaking hands on a business deal. I drove away from there trying to ignore the stiffening in my cock, wondering if I'd really felt what I thought I'd felt.

So it's just going to be me and my left hand again tonight, and if thoughts of that hot mechanic are the fuel for my fevered wanking, who's ever going to know? It's been the one highlight in my shitty week, and more than enough to weave a filthy fantasy around. That's assuming I'm not too knackered when I get in to think about pleasuring myself. Though it's been a quiet night – Rotherham on a Friday night may never be quite the screaming, puking, knicker-flashing war zone some town centres can become when the drink starts flowing, but the bad weather's either keeping people at home, or they've settled on their favourite club and stayed there, rather than hopping from one venue to the next as they otherwise might. When you've spent an hour getting your hair just right and you haven't bothered with a coat to save on cloakroom charges, you're not going to ruin your look by stepping out in a rainstorm.

Not that I mind. Some nights, it's nice not to have to intervene and separate two beered-up lads spoiling for a fight while they wait to get inside, or fend off the attentions of girls who think they can flirt their way to the head of the queue. Sometimes, it's more than just idle chat: I've had more than one phone number pushed into the pocket of my overcoat, or scrawled in eyeliner pencil on the back of my hand, so many promises of a fuck I'll never forget if only I respond. Gaz and the lads laugh when I tell them, and claim it's down to this bad boy vibe I give off, with my close-cropped hair, diamond ear stud and stubbled chin. I don't see it myself, but then I've never really been too concerned about the image I present to women.

Checking my watch, I see there's still more than 40 minutes till I come to the end of my shift. Already people are beginning to stagger out of the club in twos and threes, calling their farewells to each other in slurred voices, louder than they'd usually use, not yet adjusted to the difference between the thumping music inside and the silence on the street out here. Girls' heels clack in staccato rhythm on the pavement as they dash down the hill in the direction of the nearest minicab office. A lone car drives past, tyres hissing against the wet road surface, pulling to a long, frustrating halt at lights still set to control the flow of daytime traffic. The odd person wishes me goodnight as they leave, but most of them don't even see me; they ever only notice the door supervisor on their way inside. I can never decide whether or not I like it that way.

'Hey, Rich.' The voice at my elbow startles me. It's Tyrone, holding what looks like the brown envelope containing my wages in one big fist. There's a smile on his craggy features, mouth open wide enough to show off his gold tooth. I can't help but return the grin. As bosses go, there are far worse people to work for. 'Why don't you slope off early for once, man?' He presses the wage packet, reassuringly thick, into my hand. 'I think you've earned it, and we should be able to cope all right without you. They're hardly tearing the walls down in there …'

It's a nice gesture, and one he didn't need to make, but he must have known how disappointed I was when I rang him and told him I wouldn't be taking that couple of days' holiday I'd asked for after all. I tuck my money in my coat pocket and clap Tyrone on the shoulder, thanking him in sincere tones and telling him I'll see him tomorrow. Then, hunching deeper into my Crombie to keep the rain off me as best I can, I start trudging up the hill to where I've left my car, parked on the square in front of the Town Hall.

That's when I see it all about to kick off, the players in a nasty little tableau moving into position, even if only one of them is aware it's happening. He's the skinny little runt lurking in the alleyway by the side of the church, the perfect spot to wait for a suitable victim passing by, almost invisible in in his nondescript black hoodie and dark jeans. I don't think he's noticed me yet, and even if he had, he'd instinctively shy away from coming anywhere near me. I spend my working nights looking out for trouble, and I can handle it when it happens. And the way I carry myself reflects that. You mess with me at your peril.

The bloke across the road from me is a different matter entirely. He's got his hood up too, but the white cord of the headphones he's got jammed in his ears is visible even from this distance. On his way home, I assume, but completely oblivious to his surroundings. He might as well have "please rob me" tattooed across his forehead.

Almost without being aware I'm doing it, I quicken my pace, wanting to get near enough to prevent the inevitable confrontation. Before I've closed the gap enough, the mugger dashes out of his hiding place, and I get the briefest glimpse of a knife gleaming in the light from a street lamp as he pushes Mr Headphones up against the wall. I don't even stop to think about any threat to my own safety; all my training kicks in and I go charging over, grabbing him from behind.

The mugger doesn't know what hits him. I'm bending his wrist back on itself, forcing him to drop his weapon. He howls in pain, turns to curse at me, and I do my best to imprint his features on my memory: the sharp nose, the sallow cheeks, the scatter of acne on his forehead and chin. I'm sure I can give a decent description of him if I need to. For all that he can't weigh more than nine stone soaking wet, he's stronger than he looks, wriggling out of my grip despite my best efforts to hold on to him as I yell at Headphones to call the police. Twisting away from me, he's off down the alley, away into the night, leaving his switchblade lying on the pavement.

I could run after him, but my focus has switched from the lad to the guy he tried to rob. He pulls his hood down, and I realise I'm staring into a familiar face, that of my hot mechanic.

It takes a moment – maybe it's delayed shock – but eventually he recognises me too. 'Thanks, mate.' There's a tremor in his voice, and he leans against the wall for support.

'Did he take anything?' I ask.

He shakes his head. 'No. He was trying to get me to hand over my phone, but then you – you …'

'Well, maybe it'll teach you to look after yourself a bit better, not just go wandering round at two in the morning with your music on full blast and no idea if anyone's following you.' I'm sharper with him than maybe I mean to be, but he needs to know what a fucking stupid thing he's just done.

'Yeah, I'm sorry. A few of us have been over at a mate's house and I kind of lost track of time. And I didn't want to drive there because I knew I'd be drinking. You know how it is. I don't know what I'd have done if you hadn't been around.' His tone changes, takes on a note I haven't heard from another guy since Tony. 'God, you were amazing. Thank you so much …'

And before I can react, he's pressed his lips to mine, in

a hot, searching kiss. Adrenaline fuels his actions, I'm sure, sparked by the relief of having so narrowly escaped being robbed at knifepoint, but there's more to his response than that. He wants me not only because of what happened just now, but because of that moment in the garage yesterday.

I wasn't imagining his attraction to me, and the knowledge makes me sigh as he pushes his tongue into my mouth, revelling in the taste of him, sweet with red wine and breath mints. All thoughts of reporting what's just happened to the police melt away under the force of his kiss. His groin grinds against mine, and the bulge there is hard and all too evident. Knowing he's so turned on makes my own cock rise up in reaction.

When he finally breaks away from me, we're both panting for breath. His eyes shine.

'I only live round the corner. Come with me …'

How can I resist his invitation? I just about have the presence of mind to pick up the switchblade in a handkerchief, and stow it in my pocket; if nothing else, I can make sure there's one less knife in circulation. That on its own would make it a good night in my book, but things are going to get better from here, I can tell.

By the time we reach the terraced two-up, two-down where he lives, I've learnt that his name is Adie. More than that, I don't need to know right now. Personal history will only get in the way of acting on the lust that's threatening to drive me crazy.

We're barely through the front door, into a hallway that smells of fresh paint, before his lips are on mine again. I shrug out of my coat as we kiss, letting it lie where it falls. We make slow, shuffling progress up the stairs, shedding clothes as we go, so that by the time we reach the bedroom we've lost footwear, socks and tops.

Shirtless, his body is as good as I imagined, broad in the shoulders, tapering to lean hips that his jeans ride low on, revealing the wide white waistband of his underwear.

Pushing him back on to his bed, I wrestle him out of those jeans. He may be a good five or six inches taller than me, but I've got the strength to pin him with one hand and strip him down with the other. He doesn't object, loving the way I've taken charge.

When his shorts come down, his dick bobs up so hard it almost slaps me in the face as I bend close to his crotch. I grab it by the base, holding it steady and giving him a moment to consider all the possibilities of what I might be about to do to him. From the look on his face, seems like every one thrills him more than the last. His breathing is fast, harsh, and he can't help but thrust his hips up toward me, urging me to give him what he needs.

His eyes widen as my lips latch on to his jutting cockhead, and he moans like he can't quite believe this is happening to him. I've already considered, and dismissed, the possibility there's someone else in the house. We've made more than enough noise since we came in to wake anyone who might be sleeping, but there's been no sign of movement from any of the other rooms, and at no point has Adie tried to shush me. It's just the two of us, excited, horny and, in his case, very naked, free from any fear of interruption.

I swallow as much of him as I can, feeling the blunt head nudge against the back of my throat as he tries to push in deeper. He's eager, all jerking hips and soft grunts, and I wonder how long it's been since anyone last did this to him. Keen to come as he is, I'm not going to rush this. Letting him slip out of my mouth again, I lick from tip to base, then lower, tonguing his hairy balls before zeroing on the rosy pucker of his arsehole. He squirms a bit at first, and I wonder briefly if anyone's ever done this to him before. Doesn't try to stop me, mind, and the noises he's making start to show definite signs that he likes this, whether or not he thinks he should.

When his hole is good and wet, I slide a finger inside, pushing in and out while I go back to sucking his cock. Now he's humping his arse against the mattress in demented pleasure. He mutters something, trying to warn me he's about to come, because the next thing I know his spunk is gushing into my mouth, thick and slightly bitter tasting. Adie's apology is mumbled, but I'm not cross with him – if I was as keyed up as he clearly is, I doubt I'd have been able to say anything either.

More than anything, I need to do something about my own satisfaction. I'm so hard, my underwear is almost squeezing the life out of my cock. Adie lies there, eyes riveted to my groin as I take off the rest of my clothing, and the way he sucks in a breath at the sight of my erection makes me even more eager to bury my length inside him.

There's just one thing needs to happen before we get to that stage. 'Condom?' I ask.

'In the drawer.' He indicates the bedside cabinet with a nod of his head. There's a packet of 12 in there, the extra-strong type, along with a bottle of anal lube. Seems like there are some aspects of his personal safety he does pay attention to, after all.

Squeezing lube on to my fingers, I grease up his arse. Obligingly, he's got up on all fours so his backside is presented to me, taut and inviting. When he's slick enough to take three fingers with relative ease, I skin on the condom. Kneeling behind him, I line myself up with the target and push home. His chute is hot and tight, gripping my cock like a fist, and I can only inch in slowly.

Adie moans and hisses through his teeth, like I'm stretching him wider than he's used to, and I can't help that thrill of pride at the thought I'm the biggest he's ever taken. When I can't push myself any deeper, I take a minute to get myself used to the feeling of being engulfed by his arse.

'God, don't tease me,' Adie begs. 'Fuck me, Rich, please.'

So I do, just shallow thrusts at first but gradually building in a swift, intense rhythm that has us both gasping and sweating and hungry for more. I'm gripping his hips, banging him so hard that my balls slap against his arse cheeks with every thrust, and still he's urging me on to go faster, deeper. Then we've gone into a place beyond words, beyond thought, driven on by some basic need to take and be taken. I had no idea this was how my evening was going to end when I rocked up for work, buried to the root in the arse of a guy I barely know but who wants me with a passion I haven't experienced in so long now. But fate's funny like that, taking us places we never expected to go, and what can you do at a time like this but let it lead you where it wants?

Adie's passage seems to clutch me even tighter as my cock swells inside him, and I'm coming, pumping everything I have into the condom, almost growling in satisfaction as my balls empty.

For the first time since I left the club, I find myself thinking about Gaz and the lads, and wonder what they'd say if they knew what's happened to me tonight. They might have the great weather and the cheap booze, but I've got Adie. And I know where I'd rather be right now.

## Last Minute Treat
### by Allex K. Bell

'*Look, I'm just –*' I started, a bit too forcefully, which I immediately toned down '– trying to *apologise,* OK?'

'Apology accepted,' my lover of five years, Barry, said, sounding exasperated with me.

'It's not though, is it?'

'Not really,' he agreed flatly, as he distracted himself making a cup of tea.

'Look, how many more times have I got to say I'm sorry?'

This time he raised his voice.

'As many times as you stare openly at other guys, and tell me you'd love to drop to your knees in front of them and jack them off into your mouth, until they fill it with their scrummy cream!'

'I'm only – having a bit of *fun,* that's all.'

'But you really would *love* to do that to some of them, wouldn't you?'

'Err … No, not really!'

Barry let out a dismissive, tight-lipped hiss and started vigorously stirring the sugar into his tea.

'You're my – one and only, you know that!'

'Do I?' He sighed as he walked out of the kitchen.

'I would never do that with anyone else!'

'You'd better get it all out in your dreams then,' he said softly, sounding really fed up, 'and by the way, you're on the couch tonight.'

And with that, he threw me the spare quilt and pillow and slammed the bedroom door.

I just stood staring at it.

'Fuck!' I was angry at myself, not him.

After I'd readied the couch and slumped down under the quilt, already feeling pretty uncomfortable, I considered the latest outburst that had so upset him. It was stupid, and insensitive, and I definitely should have kept my big, fucking mouth shut!

The guy I'd commented about, Stuart, was a friend of the bar manager at our usual. I'd been checking him out all night, and when Barry wasn't around, I was sure he was giving me the eye too; he was around 23, a couple of years younger than me, was about 5 foot 10 tall, slim, athletic body, and had a cute, clean-cut face, from which his glorious smile shone out like a beacon, making me stiff between the legs, and wetting the tip of my cock.

But despite the feelings the hot young stranger had stirred in me, I shouldn't have been so open with my stares – it was completely disrespectful. And I shouldn't have said what I did either, which as I recall, was a good bit more graphic than my lover had recited, something like – *I'd love him to pump his spunk into my mouth, to flood it with his thick, scrummy, creamy spend, until he'd emptied the entire contents of his balls through my tightly sucking lips, and I'd swallowed the whole lot down into my stomach* – which was *also* pretty disrespectful!

But sometimes I can't stop myself from thinking these thoughts. Anyway, it's all very well Barry taking the moral high ground – he'd had his fun when he was younger. From what I'd heard from friends his age (nearly six years older than me), he used to really put it about; indulging in all sorts of fun and games. Whereas I, on the other hand, have hardly any sexual experience outside of our relationship – I wasn't a virgin when I met him, but I wasn't very experienced either. Sometimes I just wish I'd slept with more men before him.

Now we're together though, it's great – No, it's *fantastic!* We have amazing sex, and a lot of it too – I just sometimes wonder *what if?*

Either way, what I did tonight was wrong, and as I curled over on to my side and tucked the quilt in tight around me, I vowed to try and change, and to make it up to him as best I could. Of course, I did have an ulterior motive too, as it's going to be my birthday on Friday, and Barry always gives me the most amazing presents – not gifts, but days out, doing things I always wanted to do, but never had the means. He's amazing, really: kind, generous, loving, and he's a really good fuck too!

'Stuck in the Friday night traffic?' Barry asked, before hugging me tight, and then giving me a lovely long, and quite dirty, birthday kiss, which left me gasping a little afterwards.

'Terrible,' I sighed, still smiling stupidly.

'Never mind,' he said quietly, before adding, 'we need to get a shufty on; we're running a little late.'

Barry's excited expression betrayed something amazing he had planned for me.

'We off out somewhere?' I asked, trying to glean something out of him.

But he shook his head, his lips sealed. Instead, he ushered me into the bedroom, which was when my jaw dropped; there in front of us was a set of weekend cases, and on the handles I could see the flag of the European Union – which could only mean one thing!

'*Berlin*?' I half gasped, half pleaded.

He didn't speak, but the growing smile on his face told me it was true.

I leapt forward and hugged him really hard. Berlin was where we'd first met, both on business courses with different companies. Sex with him had been the first great sex I'd ever had. We always said we'd go back there, to relive some of the great memories, but despite both having pretty well paid jobs, we'd struggled to get ahead of the bills – or so I'd thought.

'Get showered and changed; the taxi will be here in an hour.'

I hurriedly did as he said, chatting with him about Berlin as I scrubbed myself clean, feeling so excited about what lay ahead.

When I returned to the bedroom, he held a towel wide open for me.

'Rub down, sir?' he asked, sounding like some sort of exclusive hotel employee.

'That would be very nice, thank you,' I sighed, smiling hugely, as I reversed up to him and he wrapped the towel around me.

He slid his hands all around my body, rubbing the towelling material across the entire surface of my torso: my shoulders, my back, my chest, my stomach, and then even further down – drying me, soothing me, and stimulating me too.

'That nice?' he asked softly, as I let my head loll back onto his shoulder, while he started rubbing where my muscular thighs met my crotch, teasingly close to my throbbing balls and aching cock, which I could feel was sticking right out from my body now.

'Really fucking nice!'

'How about this?' he asked, as he slipped a towel-covered fist around my cock and slowly wanked on it.

'Oh yeah,' I gasped, as I started to fuck my cock through his grip, and he started to push his growing bulge against the crack of my arse. 'Have we got time to play?'

'I think so.' His voice was almost a whisper. 'But how about trying something new?'

'I'm game,' I moaned, as I just kept rocking my hips back and forth, fucking it through his gripping fingers and the coarse weave of the towel, which was even further stimulating it.

Then, from out of nowhere, Barry pulled a blindfold up, and started securing it around my eyes.

'Somebody's all prepared.'

'Dib, dib, dib.'

*'Dob, dob, dob!'* I replied, and then we both let out a quiet, comfortable laugh.

'Be serious,' he said then, which revealed how excited he was, which made my cock lurch hard between my legs; if *he* was this excited, I was going to love whatever he was going to do to me.

As soon as the blindfold was fixed, and he was sure I couldn't see a thing, I felt him walk around in front of me.

'Sit down on the end of the bed!' he instructed softly.

As soon as I was sitting, he dropped quietly to his knees before me.

'Kiss me!' he said next, his heavy-breathing lips close to mine, sounding very excited.

I let my lips drift open, ready to receive the first touch of his lips.

His kiss was surprisingly passionate, his lips sliding and mashing roughly against mine, as his tongue slurped and licked around the insides. And then he started feather-flicking his tongue against mine, lashing it with his, as our saliva mingled and squidged back and forth. Just when I was starting to gasp helplessly, he pulled away a touch, and licked straight across the outside of my lips, peeling them open, and wetting my cheeks and chin.

'Shit, I liked that.' I smiled like a Cheshire cat, as my cock kept lurching excitedly between my legs. 'Have you been practising with someone else?'

He laughed.

'Maybe!'

I laughed back. He wouldn't do that to me – of that I was sure!

'Kiss me again.' He sighed, his excited breaths getting shorter too.

I puckered my lips again, and lifted my hands up to embrace him, and to feel for his cock.

'Ah, ah, ahh!' he cried quickly, slapping my wrist. 'No hands yet, just kissing for now, and then we'll add something else in a bit, OK?'

'You are *good* today.' I lowered my hand and rubbed at my cock a little. 'OK, I'll play by the rules.'

But then I realised something, and had a panic attack.

'Shit, what time's the taxi getting here?'

'Don't worry your pretty little head about it,' he said calmly, as he smoothed a few stray hairs back from my face. 'It's not for another two hours – I lied about the time so you got your butt in gear!'

*'Cheeky git!'* I cried loudly, and gave him a playful thump on the arm, before lowering it down to join the other one at my cock. 'All yours, baby. I'll just keep my hands *here*, out of the way!'

'That's a good boy.' He half laughed, half sighed, sounding even more turned on. 'Now give me your lips again.'

I let my mouth fall open, which he met a few seconds later with another lovely kiss, this time starting with full, wet smackers all around my mouth, before snogging me deeply, his tongue slithering around the inside of my mouth like an excited eel. His kissing was *so good,* he had me moaning helplessly into his lips, and licking back with my tongue as good as I was getting, loving the taste of the inside of his mouth – which he must have freshened up with something new, as I didn't recognise the taste.

When our kiss broke, we were both panting like crazy. I so desperately wanted to pull him to me, and to suck on his cock, but this was his game, his rules – *and I was loving it!*

I parted my lips again, willing in the next touch of his lips.

This one was much gentler, and more tender, much more like his usual kisses – which was when the penny dropped, and I gasped into his deliciously sucking and slurping mouth, before pushing him away a little.

'Oh my God, what's going on?' I shrieked, as I reached up for the blindfold – but he slapped my hand away again.

*'No peeking!'*

'Oh shit, now I'm really fucking horny,' I gasped. 'How many guests have we got for this little birthday treat?'

*'Two* guests,' Barry replied excitedly, 'ones you've admired from afar.'

'I really want to see!'

'You'll have to wait … But maybe later.'

I had so many questions to ask him about who they were, and how he set this up, but they were all forgotten for now, when a pair of fresh hands started stroking deliciously slowly along the length of my cock, as another pair busied themselves around the base and my balls – fixing on a cock-ring I think, to draw out my come.

Then I felt Barry's hand around the back of my head,

and he brought his lips – definitely *his* lips this time – close in to my ear.

'You ready for your present now, gorgeous?'

'Oh fuck, yeah!' I gasped, as the tightly gripping hand on my cock started wanking quicker, aided by a glut of spit they'd dribbled down onto their fingers, the fresh wetness and the confident grip making my shaft swell and jerk erratically.

'OK then,' he sighed, and then he clambered in to sit directly behind me on the end of the bed, his naked body hugged up close to mine, his hands wrapped around me protectively, as his own stiffness pressed hard against the crack of my ass once again.

I think he must have given some sort of nod to the other two, as almost straight away, they started what he must have planned for me.

A warm, wet mouth slipped down over the head of my cock, and started sucking on it like it was the most delicious thing in the world. A ton of filthy sounds escaped their wicked lips, as they lapped and slurped around my pulsating head for all they were worth. And then, just when I was getting used to that, they started bobbing along the top third of my cock with quick lips, driving me wild with arousal.

'Like it?' Barry asked softly, as his hands drifted upwards and he started playing with my nipples, just idly stroking and pinching at them.

'I fucking lov …' My words were cut short, when a thick, juicy cockhead slipped in through my lips, and deep into the back of my mouth.

I tried to groan my shock, and my approval, but all that escaped my stretched lips was a deep, guttural sigh, as straight away, almost automatically, I started sucking on the tasty head, squirming my lips all around it, and lavishing it with my tongue and my saliva, truly tasting the soft, velvety plum of a head, which seemed to please the owner, who moaned deeply, and started fucking it back and forth through my lips – which I was more than happy to take.

'That's it, take it deeper into your mouth,' Barry panted into my ear, the sort of salacious comment I never normally heard from him. The fact that he was so turned on by this made me even more aroused, and caused my cock to flex and jerk in the guy's mouth below me, causing him too to moan excitedly around my flesh.

'You want more?' Barry asked softly, as he flicked his tongue across my lobe. After taking a firm grip on both my nipples, he pulled them hard out from my chest, drawing delicious pain to flood there.

I just moaned and nodded around the cock in my mouth. Again, with the blindfold on, I couldn't see any sort of signal he might have given the two men, but they certainly responded straight away, the guy between my legs jamming his lips deep down the length of my cock, deep enough for my throbbing head to start pushing at the entrance to his throat, making him gag a couple of times, as the guy in my mouth started ramrodding his, fucking his cock quickly through my stretched, gasping lips.

'Yes, that's it – that's a good little cocksucker,' Barry groaned, as he pinched and twisted my nipples now, grinding his own stiff flesh hard against me, up and down my tight crack, as if he was fucking it.

I was in absolute heaven. This must have been what Barry did regularly when he was my age, before he'd found me and settled down. I'd only ever slept with one guy at a time, yet here I was, with one on my cock and another in my mouth, as my long-term lover groped me from behind, and urged us all onwards.

'Take him down your throat,' I heard him say to the guy between my legs, who I could feel smile close to the base of my shaft, before he jammed his lips even lower, the tip of my cock slipping past the tight constriction of his throat. He gurgled disgustingly around my head, as his lips wriggled and wormed around the base of my cock, his bottom lip even starting to suck and pull at my balls, stirring up a swirling, liquid heat inside them.

I cried my escalating joy around the cock in my mouth, as it fucked faster and faster through my lips, my saliva spitting and dribbling from my lips and down my chin as I did whatever I could to make the increasingly deeper penetration as lubricated as possible.

Barry was fucking his cock even harder along the crack of my arse, and had even dropped his hands down to my hips to take a good hold of me, as he spread my cheeks wide, which is when he nearly made me come on the spot.

'You want me inside you – when *he* unloads in your mouth, and *you* unload in *his?*'

Again, all I could do was nod.

Without the other two even missing a beat, I stood myself slowly up, and then, after Barry had wet my hole with his spit, and positioned his cock there, I sat back down on it.

'Oh fuckk!' I gargled around the spearing flesh in my mouth, as I sunk right down onto Barry's cock, taking his shaft and his fist of a head deep up my arse, until my crudely stretched hole was sat down around the base of his cock.

'There, that's better,' he said softly, as his cock twitched and jerked inside me, the tip already feeling pretty wet.

I went to lift up again, so I could start a fucking action

on his cock, but his hands held my hips firm.

'Just enjoy these guys,' he whispered softly, 'I'm ready to blow up your arse at any second, so you just relax, and have fun!'

*Oh my God!* My arse clenched automatically around his length at the idea of his spunk flooding into me at any second, his favourite place to unload.

My climax was close too, as the double assault of my senses was driving me wild with lust, the guy gobbling my cock down his throat drawing my spunk up, as the guy in my mouth owned it, and was using it, twitching and lurching inside my lips, feeling close to coming too.

And then I did something I didn't believe I'd have the strength of character to do – I lifted my hands to the thighs of the guy in front of me, and pushed him away! As soon as his cock-tip was clear of my gasping lips, I blurted out what I had to say.

'I need to see who it is, Barry – please!'

And then, without any further ado, I opened my lips wide again, and the guy fucked his cock straight back in, fully accepting the open invitation to use my warm, wet, willing orifice.

'You really wanna see?' Barry asked, sounding full of lust and power over me, and excited too, his cock swelling up inside my arse, really filling me up.

I nodded helplessly, as a tear rolled down my cheek from the mass of arousal taking my body.

'You want to see whose mouth is deepthroating you?'

'Yes!'

'And you want to see who's so wonderfully fucking your sweet-looking mouth?'

'Yess … Pleeasse!' I begged, as the two guys worked faster and faster on me, until I could feel my come start to really rise.

I think he knew this, and he took pity on me, and loosened the back of the blindfold.

*Quickly – quickly – quickly –* I urged silently, as my spunk started to burn in my balls, aching for its imminent release.

He lifted the soft cloth upward a touch, just enough for me to see below, through the legs of the guy standing over me. I could see that the guy deepthroating my cock was David, who Barry used to work with. His experienced eyes locked to mine, as he slurped slowly this time down my length, until his lips were buried in my pubes, and around the red ribbon they'd tied there earlier, and as my cock flexed and jerked within the tight confines of his throat.

Seeing who it was heightened my arousal, and I knew I was going to blow any second now – which was why, I think, Barry decided to pull the blindfold completely clear of my face, allowing my gaze to lift up, and see whose cock was using my mouth.

Of course – *it was Stuart!*

I remembered, that even though Barry had been upset by what I'd said about him, I could see the attraction he felt for the young stranger too, and had maybe even pictured him using my mouth as he was now, the imagery conjured up by my dirty words exciting him.

But then Barry did something I did not expect.

'Pump your spunk into his mouth, Stuart!' he gasped nastily, his cock swelling up huge inside my arse as the filthy words escaped his lips. 'Flood it with your thick, scrummy, creamy spend, until you've emptied the entire contents of your balls through his tightly sucking lips!'

Stuart and I both groaned together at this, and I felt his fucking motions stutter too.

'And if he's the dirty slut he says he is, and I *know* he

218

is,' Barry gushed about me, 'he'll swallow the whole lot down into his stomach, and suck and suck and suck some more, until he's drained you of every last drop!'

Stuart grunted, then pulled his cock back a little, before wanking vigorously along his length, tossing himself off into my mouth faster and faster and faster, until he cried out loud, and the slit in his cockhead spread wide open, and he flooded my mouth with his creamy spend.

'That's it,' Barry grunted, as his cock flexed inside me once more, 'fill his mouth to overflowing!'

Stuart did just that, angling his spraying tip around the inside of my mouth, pumping jet after jet of scalding hot spunk into my mouth, coating my tongue, splattering the roof of my mouth, and making a filthy, sticky puddle in the back of my mouth.

'Now swallow it down, slut!' he spat finally.

As I did as he ordered, gulping down Stuart's delicious, thick, sticky spend as quickly as I could. My cock lurched in David's mouth, and he too sighed with joy, as I started unloading my cream down *his* throat. At almost exactly the same time, Barry pressed down on my hips, keeping his cock locked inside me, as it exploded inside my arse, flooding my innards with an unbelievable amount of spunk that just kept coming and coming, his cock jerking and straining inside me as it did, as I swallowed and swallowed the sticky mess in my mouth, and ejaculated the full contents of my balls into the willing mouth on my cock, until, finally, all four of us collapsed, totally drained and completely exhausted.

'Why did you do that for me?' I asked, as we cuddled up under the sheets later, the other two long gone. 'You hate me even looking at other guys!'

'If it's going to happen, I'd rather pick out who you're

with – better that than you get frustrated and go off with a total stranger.'

'Oh, OK ... Thanks!' I was still in a bit of a daze about the whole experience.

But then a nagging thought formed, which jumped into full clarity.

'Berlin!' I shrieked.

Barry let out a wry laugh.

'We've got to save a bit longer for that – I just wanted you distracted while we finalised things.'

'Thank you,' was all I could say, before a smile split my lips, and I quickly added, 'I'll try to do the same for you on your birthday, if you like.'

'Oh no, you don't!' he shrieked.